FRIENDS TO THE END

This Large Print Book carries the
Seal of Approval of N.A.V.H.

FRIENDS TO THE END

SHELLEY SHEPARD GRAY

THORNDIKE PRESS
A part of Gale, a Cengage Company

Farmington Hills, Mich • San Francisco • New York • Waterville, Maine
Meriden, Conn • Mason, Ohio • Chicago

Copyright © 2019 by Shelley Shepard Gray.
The Walnut Creek Series.
Thorndike Press, a part of Gale, a Cengage Company.

Thorndike Press® Large Print Christian Fiction.
The text of this Large Print edition is unabridged.
Other aspects of the book may vary from the original edition.
Set in 16 pt. Plantin.

LIBRARY OF CONGRESS CIP DATA ON FILE.
CATALOGUING IN PUBLICATION FOR THIS BOOK
IS AVAILABLE FROM THE LIBRARY OF CONGRESS

ISBN-13: 978-1-4328-6291-6 (hardcover)

Published in 2019 by arrangement with Gallery Books, an imprint of Simon & Schuster, Inc.

Printed in Mexico
1 2 3 4 5 6 7 23 22 21 20 19

Give all your worries and cares
to God, for He cares about you.

— 1 Peter 5:7

The best exercise for the heart
is to bend down and help
someone.

— Amish Proverb

ONE

The first time I went to the Clarks' house was with my older brother, Andy. He was twelve and I was ten. Back then, I was fairly certain my big brother could do no wrong.

February

Andy Warner *almost* hadn't glanced at his phone. He was down in Naples, Florida, with his parents and two of his father's golf buddies and was just about to walk into the grill at some crazy-expensive golf club when his cell phone vibrated.

Usually he would have ignored it, but his parents and the men had been talking about the stock market for the last hour — they wouldn't miss him for a couple of minutes.

Just as he excused himself from the group, his phone vibrated again. Walking toward the front doors, he thumbed the screen. His little sister, Tricia, wouldn't have called him for no reason.

"Hey, Trish," he said as he slid his sunglasses back over his eyes. "How's all the snow? Are you finally wishing you'd given in and come to Florida with Mom and Dad?" No matter how hard he'd tried to convince his sister that heading down to Florida for the long Presidents' Day weekend would be good for her, his twenty-year-old sister had steadfastly refused.

"Oh, Andy. You have no idea."

He was about to tease her again when something in her voice made him stop. "What's going on?"

"I'm in trouble."

The connection was breaking up. Hoping to hear her better, Andy strode toward the edge of the half-filled parking lot. As he stood on the dark pavement, heat radiating from it even in the middle of February, there was no one around to overhear. "What happened?"

"The power is out in the cabin and it's snowing like crazy. The weather reports are bad, too," she said in a rush, one word tumbling over the other. "I don't think my car can make the drive back. It's freezing, it's going to be dark in a couple of hours, and the only way I can charge my phone is to go sit in the car."

Feeling the headache that he'd been fighting off and on for the last six months come rolling back, Andy rubbed between his eyes. "You went out to the cabin by yourself? Did Mom and Dad know you were heading out there? I sure didn't."

She paused. "I didn't tell anyone I was coming out here."

Their family's cabin was nestled in the woods about ninety minutes from their home in Walnut Creek, Ohio. Their grandparents had built it when their dad was just a kid.

Over the years his parents had fixed it up until it resembled something out of one of his mother's *Midwest Living* magazines. It had two bedrooms, a huge stone fireplace, and granite countertops in the kitchen. All of them loved hanging out there, hiking, fishing, or simply doing nothing at all.

But even though the place had every modern convenience and was gorgeous, it was still secluded — really secluded. In addition, the narrow, winding road leading up to it had tripped up more than one driver in the middle of the summer.

But in the dead of winter? It bordered on treacherous. Fear for her ratcheted up his tone. "Trish, what were you —"

She cut him off, her voice sounding pinched. "Andy, believe it or not, I didn't call so you could yell at me from some beach in Florida. Chew me out all you want when you get home. But right now I need your help." She took a deep breath. "What should I do? Do you think I should try to brave the roads and go back?"

Concern slammed into his chest. Tricia might be twenty years old and a grown woman to the rest of the world, but to him she was still the little girl who used to tag along behind him and his friends. "Give me a sec. Let me think." He knew what he would do — he'd take the chance and start driving.

But this was Tricia.

After another second or two, Tricia made an impatient noise. "Can you think quicker? It's snowing so much, I'm afraid I'm going to lose our connection. You know how spotty it is out here."

She wanted him to spout off the right advice just like that? Andy mentally rolled his eyes. He was starting to have a whole new dose of respect for his parents. Was this what their lives had been like when he was a teenager and getting into trouble? Memories of him calling home in need of help taunted him like a bully.

"Look, no judgments, but why did you call me instead of Mom or Dad? How about I run inside and get —"

"Mom's been threatening to make me move back home and finish college online or something. She said I've had too much drama and that something is always going wrong with me."

Their mom was right. Tricia was a junior at Bowling Green State University, but even he knew that his smart little sister was a walking disaster. She'd had difficult roommates, lost her keys and student ID, ran out of money, and never thought things through. How one girl could be so flighty and still make the dean's list while majoring in applied mathematics was beyond him.

"So you don't want them to know you're stuck up in the cabin?"

"Absolutely not."

He began to pace, working up a sweat. "Are you in trouble? Do you have wood and water?"

"The water's fine. For some reason, the well hasn't given out. I've got some granola bars, cereal, and milk, too. But I'm stuck, Andy." Her voice quivered. "You know I wouldn't have called if I wasn't so stressed out. I can only find a couple of candles and two flashlights but no batteries. It's really bad out here."

Racking his brain, he tried to think of who would drop everything to help Tricia out. Exhaling, he realized he knew seven people. The other members of the Magnificent Eight. His best friends.

He was closer than close to these seven other men and women, thanks to the bond they'd formed back when they were toddlers. They'd vowed to be there for each other no matter what — and, amazingly, that loyalty had never wavered.

The best part about the group, for Tricia at least, was that some of the Eight were Amish. They didn't need good roads to travel on; they could use a sleigh and horses. They didn't need electricity, either. They made do without electricity all the time.

But what was most important was that both he and Tricia could trust any of them. Though she was never part of the Eight, she knew each of them really well.

And right then, he knew who to track down first. Logan lived north of Walnut Creek and knew all the back roads to the cabin. If anyone could make it there, it was him. "I'm going to call Logan Clark, Tricia. He'll get you."

"Logan?" Her voice softened with relief. "Do you really think he'd come out here for me?"

"Of course. He knows the cabin, too. So sit tight. He'll drop everything to be there."

"I hope he answers his house phone. He's New Order, right?"

"Yep." The Clarks were New Order Amish, which meant that they had a single house phone. One of the many people who lived there

17

would answer it and tell Logan about Tricia. "Listen, if for some reason I can't get ahold of him, I'll call someone else in the Eight. No matter what, you won't have to worry. Expect company to arrive in three or four hours."

She sniffed. "Thanks, Andy. What would I ever do without you?"

He laughed. "Don't worry about that. I'm not going anywhere. Now, let me call Logan and get back to Dad before he comes looking for me."

"Okay. Thanks again, Andy."

"Chin up, Trish," he reassured her, ready to find her help as soon as possible. "Go light one of those candles you found and read a book or something. Try to relax. It will be all right."

Still fighting his headache, he thumbed down his list of contacts and dialed Logan's number, smiling when his buddy picked up.

"Hello?"

"Hey, Logan, it's Andy. I'm really glad you picked up and not one of your siblings."

"Well, I'm really wonderin' why you are on the phone. I thought you were in Florida."

"I am, but I just got a call from Trish. Listen, I need a favor."

"Name it," he said.

He breathed a sigh of relief. Everything was going to be okay now. Tricia was going to be taken care of.

"Andy?" his dad called out.

Covering the mouthpiece, he turned to his father. "Sorry, Dad. There's an emergency at work. I'll be right there."

Looking relieved, his dad walked back inside. As soon as he was gone, Andy filled Logan in on Tricia and asked him to drop everything to rescue her.

Just like he'd had to back when they were twelve years old.

"I'll head out to get her within the hour. I'll bring supplies, too, in case something happens."

"If you want to bring someone else with you, that's fine with me. Trish sounded like a wreck."

"We'll see. Try not to worry."

"*Danke,* Logan," Andy said, using the Pennsylvania Dutch word for *thank you* to emphasize his relief.

"*Ack,* it's nothing. It's what friends are for. Ain't so?"

Andy smiled. "Absolutely," he said as he hung up and walked back inside the club. Though his head was pounding and he didn't feel good about keeping this secret from his parents, he believed in Logan and the strength of the Eight as much as he believed in God.

He really was blessed to have such an amazing group of friends.

Two

Back then, Andy and I weren't all that close. If you want to know the truth, we still really aren't. We're too different, I suppose. He's always been about his friends, his plans, and a good time.

Me?

Even back then, I was just trying my best to keep up.

Three hours had passed since Tricia called her brother. Since that time, she'd changed from the ratty sweats she'd been wearing to black leggings, a thick pale-pink pullover, and Uggs. She brushed her hair and even put on a little mascara and lip gloss. She supposed all of that was vain and unnecessary, but since she already felt stupid, she figured she might as well not look like a wreck, too.

From there, she decided to clean up the cabin. She straightened the living room, folded blankets, and hand washed and dried the dishes she'd been using. Next she laid a new fire and took out the trash.

Oh, and she looked out the window at least forty-seven times.

She knew it was that many times because about two hours ago, when she began to worry that Logan might not come after all, she started counting.

Thirty minutes after that, she started pacing, telling herself it was in a sad effort to keep warm, but really it was because she'd learned to do a number of things like that to dispel her nervous energy.

A long time ago she came to understand that, while Andy Warner excelled at always having all the friends and all the answers, she'd always been very, very good at messing up.

She'd given up wondering why God had doled out His gifts in such a lopsided way. Maybe He had a sense of humor?

Every time Tricia was unwise

enough to complain to her mother about how she'd never had a group of friends like Andy and was always trying to crawl her way out of some crisis, her mother had shaken her head in dismay.

And then proceeded to remind Tricia that she had plenty of gifts her older brother didn't.

Using her fingers to help drive her point home, Mom had recounted Tricia's attributes in a way that would have made most people squirm. First, Tricia had been given an ability to memorize information effortlessly, which made school fairly easy for her. God had also given her a wealth of pleasing features. She had long, thick, brown hair, brown eyes, and smooth skin that had hardly known a blemish. And while she'd never been especially thin, she certainly wasn't obese or anything. Just normal.

Of course, Mom had called her pretty.

Even though Tricia had rolled her eyes and reminded her mother that high test scores and good looks weren't everything, her mother often scoffed and said that only a girl who had been blessed with both would say such things.

Embarrassed, Tricia had learned to keep her mouth shut but would have gladly traded some of those looks for the ability to make friends easily. She would have gladly given back her string of honor rolls and academic awards for a sliver of common sense.

And now, here she was, standing next to a window in an empty cabin in the middle of a snowstorm. Still struggling with her poor choices and self-doubts.

"One day you're going to learn to think ahead, Tricia Warner," she said to the empty room. "Maybe even look at a weather report before you take off on your own into the woods."

The words seemed to echo back at her, taunting her with her own insecurities and pain when she glanced out the window again . . . and then spied a glimmer of light in the distance. The cavalry had arrived. Or at least one of the members of the Magnificent Eight. As she watched the light brighten, she gripped the window frame, feeling the same mixture of anticipation and dread that she'd felt when she called Andy.

Because if there were any people in the world who knew her faults almost as well as Andy and herself, it was the Eight, and most especially Logan Clark.

Deciding to go out and greet Logan — or whoever it was who'd shown up — Tricia put on a coat, mittens, and a hat. And she vowed right then and there that she would do her best to keep her mouth shut while her rescuer chewed her out for being so stupid to come here all alone.

She'd keep her chin up, say she

was sorry and grateful for their trouble, and would listen to a lecture the whole way home. Anything would be better than being stuck in this cabin all alone for another hour.

Feeling as prepared as she possibly could be, she walked outside and waved to the approaching sleigh and pair of horses. As it got closer, she saw that a lantern was keeping the driver company on the bench. He was also bundled up like a small child sent out to play. He had on a knit cap, a thick black scarf, a wool coat, and gloves. Actually, if she didn't know his posture and blue eyes so well, she might not have even recognized him.

Though she knew she should be

feeling nothing but relief, Tricia was currently feeling a little sick.

For some reason, though Andy had said he was going to call Logan, she hadn't imagined that he would actually come.

Okay, maybe she'd cautiously hoped that it would be someone else besides her secret crush.

Yes, the Lord really did have a sense of humor. A wicked good one.

There she was, standing out in the snow, dressed in stretchy black pants that were far too tight, fur-lined boots, an ivory stocking hat and matching mittens, and a dove-gray nylon coat. Even from a distance he could see that her brown eyes were studying him intently.

He also noticed that her lips had a swipe of pink gloss on them. Or maybe he was imagining that last part because he'd stared at those lips far too much over the last few years.

Lord, help me, he silently prayed. *Help me be the friend Tricia needs instead of the man who can't seem to stop thinking about her at the worst possible times.*

"Hey, Logan!" She held up a hand, waving hello.

As he tugged on the horses' leads and slid to a stop, Logan raised a hand, too, all the while reminding himself to remember just who beautiful Tricia Warner was — Andy's little sister. She was also spoiled, silly, and *Englisch*. All four of those things should've been enough for him to keep his thoughts about her to a minimum. But now, like it had always been, none of those things seemed to matter when he was within two feet of her.

Fact was, he was smitten.

For about the thirty-third time, Logan wished he had ignored the phone when Andy rang. Andy would have called someone else. Marie or John B. or even Harley could have come up here to rescue Tricia instead, and he could have stayed safely away.

But it seemed that wasn't meant to be.

Feeling like he was tumbling

down a hill, he got out of the sleigh and greeted her.

"Hiya, Tricia. How are you doing?" Even in the dim twilight, he could see that her cheeks had pinkened.

"If you mean how am I doing besides being embarrassed that my brother had to call you for help and that you had to drive out here in a snowstorm to come to my rescue?" She rolled her eyes. "I'm great. How are you?"

Him? Oh, he was staring at her lips again and ashamed of that fact. "Cold," he said instead.

Those perfect lips parted, and pain flashed in her eyes. "I'm so sorry."

He could be such a jerk. *"Nee —"*

"I don't know what I was thinking. Of course you're freezing," she added in a rush. "Come inside. I have a fire going." Before he could say another word, she added awkwardly, "Or do you just want to turn around? If so, I can hurry and get my things together."

"*Nee,* Tricia. Don't hurry on my account. It was a longer trip up here than I had anticipated. I need a break."

"Oh! Good." She smiled before looking hesitant again. "I mean, of course you do. Well, come on in. The heat is off but it's a whole lot warmer inside than out here."

"I need to tend to the horses first." Pointing to the shed off to the side of the cabin, he said, "Let me unhitch them and let them rest for an hour or two."

In a rush she started toward them. "Of course. I'll help you."

He held out a hand to stop her. "Do you have experience with horses, Tricia?"

"No." Looking at him shyly, she said, "I mean, not beyond petting them when I've visited your family's barn."

She was adorable.

And there went his best of intentions, melting away like snowflakes on his skin. Feeling himself soften toward her, realizing he was now thinking about pulling her into his arms and holding her close, Logan stepped back. "I won't need your help," he said, his voice sounding harsher than he intended. "Go on inside and get warm. I'll be there when I can."

Looking like she'd just been firmly put in her place, Tricia blinked, then turned around and walked inside.

The moment the cabin's front door closed behind her, Logan walked to Pet's side and started guiding him and his sister to the shed.

Pet neighed, pawing at the snow.

"I hear ya, buddy, and I completely agree," he murmured. "Being here alone with Tricia Warner is a recipe for trouble."

When Priss nickered softly, Logan reached out and patted her soft brown neck, thick with its winter coat. "You're right. I should know better and shouldn't be thinking the things I am. But I'm only human, you see."

Realizing that the temperature had dropped further and the sky looked even more ominous, he amended his earlier thoughts. It wasn't just being alone with Tricia that was cause for concern. He had a feeling the weather was about to take a turn for the worse.

THREE

"Actually, Andy would have never taken me to the Clarks' house if he had a choice."

"That's right, Priss," Logan said as he guided his second horse into the dilapidated stall. "I know it ain't much, but it covers your head, *jah*? This shed is bigger than I remember and not all that chilly. It's a blessing that a rancher owned this property before the Warners, too. Otherwise you'd be standing in the cold. All things considered, I reckon it could be worse."

But instead of looking mollified, Pet blew out a burst of air from the stall next door, showing his disdain for the surroundings.

"Why does this attitude not surprise me?" Logan murmured as he patted the horse's forehead. "At least I found you some water and brought you some *havvah* from home. You won't starve. Count your blessings, *gaul.*"

Pet responded by pawing the ground. He did look far more contrite, though, which caused Logan to grin. He loved this pair of horses, he really did.

He'd accompanied his older brother and father three years ago to the horse auction in Mount

Hope and had fallen in love at first sight with Pet and Priscilla. They'd been raised by the Schrocks, known to everyone for providing quality horseflesh. That wasn't a surprise.

What had taken everyone off guard, though, was Meyer Schrock's insistence that the pair be purchased together. He'd said that the horses had an unusual affection for each other and would no doubt be difficult if separated.

More than one man had scoffed at the idea and said that he'd discipline the horses until they behaved on their own. But Meyer had refused to accept any bids from those men.

In the midst of it all, Logan's father had seen something he liked in the pair. After telling Meyer that, even going so far as to share that he understood the need for horses to be near their siblings given that he had six *kinner* of his own, *Daed* had purchased the pair for a song.

That was how his family had come to own a pair of buggy horses with atrocious names. But for what it was worth, Meyer had been exactly right. Both Pet and Priscilla were mighty *gut* horses. Hardworking and agreeable. Furthermore, they didn't mind working separately, as long as they were kept in stalls next to each other at night.

That was something else all the Clark *kinner* could relate to. They'd all shared rooms and were used to the companionship.

After giving Priss her water and a handful of oats, Logan knew he couldn't put off the inevitable any longer. Grabbing the large canvas duffel bag he'd loaded onto the sleigh in case the storm worsened, he turned toward the door.

He needed to go into the cabin and see Tricia. No doubt she was sitting in the dark and wondering what was taking him so long. Maybe even feeling sad because he'd refused her offer of help.

If his older brother Eli had heard him, he would have cuffed Logan on the back of the head for making her feel bad about the offer in the first place. Logan would've deserved it, too. Clark men didn't go out of their way to embarrass people. Especially young women who were in need of their help.

So he really did need to go inside.

To say he was dreading it was putting it mildly. Not because Tricia was difficult or annoying. *Nee,* the problem was with himself, not her. He simply didn't know how to act around Trish anymore. Not since she'd smiled at him about three years ago and he realized he hadn't been able to stop thinking about her since.

Squaring his shoulders, he left the shelter of the shed and headed to the cabin, lugging the canvas duffel on one of his shoulders. The wind had picked up, making the snow fall even faster. The clouds had darkened in the distance, too.

It was becoming mighty obvious that they weren't going to be heading anywhere anytime soon.

After briefly entertaining the idea of knocking first, he opened the door and stepped inside.

Sure enough, Tricia was sitting on the edge of the couch, arms wrapped around her middle, looking miserable.

"Sorry I took so long," he said as he unwound his sodden scarf and slipped off his coat and boots. "It took me a bit to get the horses watered."

She got to her feet, which were now clad only in thick pink socks. "Do you need more water? There's a pitcher in the kitchen and the plumbing works fine. I could fill it up and take it out."

"There's no need," he said as he hung his coat on the hook by the door. "Like I said, the horses are taken care of. Pet and Priscilla are fine."

"Oh." Still standing, she searched his face as if she was looking for more information than he had to give. "I bet you're freezing."

"I'm all right."

"Why don't you go stand by the fire and I'll bring you something. Um, would you like a Diet Coke?"

He almost laughed. Of course Tricia would have no power and be sitting in the dark but have a ready supply of her favorite soda. "*Danke,* but I think I'll pass for now."

She pursed her lips, obviously uneasy.

Reminding himself that she was Andy's little sister, Logan kept his expression impassive. He would only make things worse if he allowed anything he was feeling to show.

He sat down, silently encouraging her to do the same. When she sat, he leaned back, pretending to feel more at ease than he actually did. "When did you get here?"

"Yesterday. And before you tell me that it was a dumb idea to come up here by myself, believe me, I know."

"All I heard from Andy was that you were stuck in the cabin because of the snowstorm. He didn't say anything else."

Hope flared in her eyes. "Really?"

Unable to help himself, he brushed a knuckle against her cheek. "Truly. Talk to me, Trish. Why did you come up here? Why are you here instead of on vacation with your family?"

"I just couldn't do it again. I couldn't hang out with my parents and my brother and pretend that everything was fine."

"Why would you need to pretend? Couldn't you have simply told them the truth?"

"If I was with your family, maybe I could. But with mine?" She shook her head slowly. "Our family doesn't work that way."

Logan let this sink in for a moment, hoping that some story Andy had shared in the past would make her words suddenly make sense. But they didn't. "How does your family work?"

Her eyes widened, then she smirked. "My parents believe in landing on one's feet. They don't expect any of us to be perfect, but if we make mistakes, they want to discuss them and make a plan."

"Really? That doesn't sound like Andy."

"I don't know if it does or doesn't. All I know is that he's good at it." She leaned back, folding one long leg under the other. "And before you ask, I had a really bad semester up at Bowling Green. I took twelve hours, and managed to earn one B, two Cs, and a D plus."

"Ouch."

"Yeah. My grades were awful. And then there was the fact that I broke up with Emerson."

"Who was he?" It was a struggle to keep his voice even. "Your boyfriend?"

"Yep." She got to her feet. "Emerson and I had been together for eight months."

"*Acht* months?" How had he not known that?

Glancing his way, she nodded. "That might not seem like a lot to you, but for me? It was practically an eternity."

"An eternity's a long time," he murmured, already hating Emerson even though he knew better than to hate anyone.

She blinked, then laughed. "I know one thing. It's a whole lot longer than Emerson and I lasted, that's for sure."

"What happened to the two of you?" And why did he even want to know the details?

"I learned the hard way that he wasn't nearly as nice as I thought he was," she said as she sat back down next to him.

"And then?" he asked, trying not to imagine everything that this Emerson could have done.

"Then?" A new, bleaker expression appeared on her face. "Oh, then everything fell apart."

And just like the storm outside the cabin's walls, Logan realized that so much of what he'd imagined happening to Tricia was actually much worse.

FOUR

Andy and Logan and a couple of their friends had made plans for that day. Since Logan is one of six kids, Andy assumed I could hang out with one of his sisters. I don't know why; I hardly knew them at all. I was sure it was going to be awkward. I was right.

As the silence stretched between them, Tricia realized that she'd just shared more with Logan about Emerson than she had with either her parents or her brother. Or her roommate at school.

How did he have that effect on her?

"I'm sorry," she muttered, jumping to her feet again. "Here you've come all this way to help me get through this storm in the dark, and all I've been doing is telling you about my problems."

His blue eyes softened. "I asked, remember?" Taking off his knit hat, Logan ran a hand through his dark blond hair. Almost as if he was as uneasy as she was.

That probably was the case. Shifting her weight to one foot, she said, "Even I know there's a difference between asking a basic question and expecting a simple answer and getting subjected to someone's whole life story."

"It was hardly that, Trish. Besides, I know most of your story anyway."

"You know Andy's story."

"I might know more than you think," he said cryptically. Still gazing at her intently, he said, "For the record, I'm glad you told me. It was obvious you needed to tell someone about that man."

She folded her arms over her chest. "I guess I did," she said, hoping he believed that she'd told him everything. "I do feel better. I didn't feel comfortable talking to my parents about everything."

He grinned. "I suppose not."

Maybe it was his calm, unflappable manner. Maybe it was simply because she was finally telling someone about her problems. Whatever the reason, instead of shutting up, she just kept trying to explain herself. "I thought coming to this cabin and being on my own was the right thing to do. That having time to sort out my thoughts would help me think about Emerson and my plans for the future more clearly. Unfortunately, all I've been doing is worrying about getting stuck."

"How did you get out of the trip to Florida, anyway? I thought your parents would've pushed you to go. Or Andy, at least, would have tried to persuade you to go so he'd have company."

Logan had a point. She and Andy loved their parents dearly, but they were sure they were always right and had never been shy about saying so. "Oh, my parents wanted me there, but I told them I had to work. And Andy? Well, I think he understood."

"You had to work in Walnut Creek? But it's February. Don't you have to get on back to school?"

"We got a whole week off for Presidents' Day. And to answer your question, I work over in Charm. I've got a great job at Kinsinger's. I've been working there off and on for years."

"The lumber mill?"

She smiled. "Don't look so surprised. I work in the café and in the retail store. Sometimes they even let me teach kids a couple of classes."

"What kind?"

"Simple arts and crafts projects," she explained, realizing that he'd been asking her about her job in order to get her to settle down. She shook her head. Only Logan could so easily calm her and make all her worries seem suddenly manageable.

Realizing that she'd stopped mid-explanation, she added, "When I head those classes up, they're on the main calendar so they aren't easy to cancel. That's why I told my parents I couldn't get away."

"Do you truly have classes to teach?"

"Well . . ."

"You lied." His lips quirked.

"Yeah," she said softly. "Well, I mean I just didn't tell them the whole truth." When he scoffed, she smiled back at him. "I was going to stay out here for three or four days, just to get my head back on straight. Then I really do have a class I'm scheduled to teach. I couldn't have gone to Florida even if I'd wanted to."

"You are too hard on yourself. Believe it or not, I wasn't judging you. Just trying to understand."

"Thanks for that. And I'm sorry. I don't know why I'm always thinking the worst these days."

"I don't know, either . . . Oh, Trish."

"What?"

"That." He made a turning motion with his hand. "Look out the window."

When she did, she wished she hadn't.

They were now in the middle of a full-fledged blizzard. In just the space of thirty minutes, the sky had darkened, and the snow had increased to the point that it was nearly impossible to see anything but a swirling mass of white outside the window.

"Logan, I don't know whether to be thankful that you and your horses got here in time or to apologize to you again for being out in it in the first place."

"Be thankful, always." But his words seemed more like rote than from the heart. Frowning, he walked over to the window and stared. "It's mighty bad out."

She realized then that she'd been lying to herself about the weather. "We're not going to be able to leave, are we?"

"*Nee.* Not today. If it gets as bad as I fear, we might not even be able to leave *meiya,* either."

"Will the horses be okay out there in the shed overnight?" She knew that her dad had wanted to keep the stalls on the inside like the rancher before, but it still wasn't much of a barn.

He nodded. "Pet and Priscilla should be just fine. I noticed that the walls were sturdier and thicker than they looked. They'll keep out most of the wind and snow."

Thinking about the cold, she remembered that she hadn't gone out to the woodpile since yesterday morning. "I better bring in some logs so we don't freeze."

"I'll do it. Where are they?"

"Under the tarp, just around the corner. Luckily, there's a lot of wood to burn."

"That is a blessing." He was still staring at the snow falling down. "We need to make some phone calls, too. I need to let my family know what's going on, and you should call Andy."

"You're right. He's probably wondering why I haven't called him yet and making a new plan for me in case I don't." She shook her head. "It's amazing how Andy is sure he can manage things even from the beach."

Logan turned around and grinned. "If he didn't try to manage things, then he wouldn't be the Andy I know."

She got her phone and turned it back on, then walked to the kitchen and watched the bars on the screen slowly appear. Progress was slow, but at last she got three bars — the minimum she knew she needed to get reception. "You can use it now." She held it out. "It works best in here, I don't know why."

"You go first."

"No, Andy can wait. Your family will be worried about you."

"Danke." He tapped his number and held it up to his ear. Tricia

watched his frown ease when someone picked up. "Who's this? Kevin?
Hiya." He paused. "*Jah.* I made it
to the cabin, obviously. But the
shtoahm is bad. Snow's comin'
down something awful." He paused
again. "*Nee,* don't worry. We're
fine. Tricia and I are going to build
a fire and eat hot dogs."

"Hot dogs?" she mouthed.

He grinned and shrugged. "*Jah.*
S'mores, too," he added with a
laugh. "Tell *Mamm* and *Daed* not
to worry."

After he hung up, he said, "Let
me give Elizabeth Ann a call, too.
I'd feel better if someone else in
the Eight knew what was going on."

Tricia nodded but her insides
knotted again.

Carefully dialing Elizabeth's number, he waited, and then left a message. "E. A., it's Logan. Listen, Andy called me and asked me to help his sister. She was stuck out in their cabin. Remember that one? The one where we all went for Andy's and John's birthdays? Anyway, the snow has gotten worse, so I'm gonna stay out here until I can get her home safe. My family knows, I just wanted someone else to know, too. Let the rest of the Eight know, will ya? *Danke.*"

Now not only did Andy, Logan, and his family know she'd been so foolish, but Elizabeth Ann and whoever else she told would, too.

She felt completely betrayed. "Why does everyone else need to know about this, Logan?"

"So they can pray for us," he said simply.

She suddenly felt even younger and more ungrateful. "Oh. I . . . I didn't know you guys did stuff like that."

His eyebrows rose. "You didn't know I prayed?"

"No. I mean, yes, of course I knew you prayed," she said, feeling more flustered by the second. "I didn't realize that all of you prayed for each other." Andy sure hadn't mentioned that. Had he?

When Logan continued to study her, almost as if he was trying to come up with the right thing to say, she held out a hand. "I'd better call Andy now."

"*Jah.* Sure." Without another word, he handed the phone to her. Then, instead of moving to the side to at least pretend to give her privacy, Logan stayed right next to her while she called.

Unlike Elizabeth, Andy answered right away. "It's about time you called."

Tricia inwardly groaned. This was so like him, always so certain of everything. Always so ready to make sure she never forgot that he was her big brother. "I've been a little busy, Andy."

"Whatever. I was starting to worry." On its heels, he continued, his voice a little more tentative. "Everything's okay, right? The ride home with Logan went well?"

"Uh, no."

"What happened?"

"Actually, there's a problem."

"What?" he asked again, his voice turning more panicked. "I know it can be hard traveling in that buggy, but —"

"It wasn't the buggy, Andy."

"What happened?" Again, before she had a moment to even attempt to answer him, he fired off another question. "Did you guys get stuck in the snow? Or wait — did Logan not get there?"

"Logan got here just fine." Practically feeling Logan's gaze resting on her, she tried to sound more carefree than she felt. "He's, um, standing right next to me."

"Where are you?"

Andy's voice sounded so strained, she could almost see the confusion on his face. Darting a glance at Logan, she said, "We're still at the cabin, Andy."

"Still?"

"Settle down and let me speak. And, for once, listen. Okay?"

"I'm listening. What happened?"

"Well, first of all, it took a while for Logan to get here. The weather isn't just bad, it's really bad. Then we had to let the horses rest. But now the storm's gotten worse." Glancing at Logan again, she said, "We're not going to be able to leave tonight." There was no way she was going to warn him that it might be even longer.

Her brother mumbled something

under his breath before speaking. "Trish, come on. How bad can the storm be?"

"It can be pretty darn bad, Andy," she retorted, using the last of her patience. "I didn't call you to ask for permission, by the way. I called to let you know what was going on. We're going to stay here tonight and leave in the morning if the weather has cleared."

"Hey, besides Logan, who else is there?"

She was getting more than a little annoyed with these questions. "Uh, the horses."

"Tricia, besides the horses."

"There's no one here besides Logan, me, and the horses." Raising her voice, she said, "Honestly,

Andy, what did you expect? For Logan to bring the rest of the Eight here? And why? So we could have a chaperone? You know I'm twenty, right? That I'm in college and there are actually boys wandering around Bowling Green that I talk to on occasion?"

Logan held out his hand. "Let me talk to him."

Tricia knew Andy would probably appreciate talking to Logan, but even the idea of handing over the phone like a child didn't sit with her well. She shook her head. "I've got this," she hissed.

"What have you got?" Andy asked.

Oh, brother. "Nothing." Staring at Logan, she said, "Everything is fine here." Well, besides being stuck in the cabin with her childhood crush.

"Are you sure? Maybe I shouldn't have asked one of the guys to come get you. Maybe I should have called the sheriff or something."

Now he was just being ridiculous. "I don't think Logan and I are going to fall into bed together just because we're all alone, Andy."

Beside her, she heard Logan suck in a mouthful of air. He reached for the cell phone. "Tricia, I *canna* believe you said that," he blurted, his voice as hard as she'd ever heard it. "Hand me the —"

She covered the bottom of her cell. "No." Lowering her hand, she murmured, "Andy, trust me, okay?"

"Of course I trust you. I just worry." He sighed. "I wish you had come down to Naples. If you had, you wouldn't be in this situation, you know."

"I know, but I needed a break. Now, I really appreciate you calling Logan to come help me. I also know you're worried. But you need to relax. If you don't, Mom and Dad are going to wonder what's got you so spun up."

He sighed. "About that. I think I should let them know what's going on."

"You'd better not."

"Tricia —"

"I've kept your secrets, Andy," she interrupted. "Mom and Dad still don't know you got that warning your freshman year of college. I'm the one who confiscated that note and forged their signatures. And don't even get me started about prom."

"Why do you always bring up prom?" he asked, his voice matching hers.

"Because I have to remind you now and again that I've always been there for you. I might be a wreck right now, but you aren't perfect, either. Don't betray me."

After a pause, he said, "If you aren't home safe in twenty-four hours, I'm going to have to let them know."

"No, if I'm not back home within forty-eight hours, I'll give them a call myself."

He laughed. "Boy, you grew up, didn't you?"

Feeling kind of proud of herself, she smiled. "I did."

"I don't know when that happened."

"I'm starting to think it happened a while ago, Andy. It was just that nobody ever wanted to believe it." Maybe not even herself. "Now, I love you, but I've gotta go."

"Okay, bye. Be careful."

"I will. Bye, now."

When at last she clicked off, she turned to Logan with a smile.

He, however, was definitely not smiling back at her. His face looked irritated, and his arms were folded across his chest. "You don't think we'll be going to bed together? What the devil does that mean?"

Oops. It looked like she'd just ticked off the one person who could make her life easier.

FIVE

To make matters worse, the whole time we were walking over to the Clarks', Andy gave me warnings about what I shouldn't say or do when I got to their house. By the time we entered their front yard, I was a nervous wreck.

Andy stared at the screen of his cell phone for almost five minutes after Tricia disconnected. He hadn't been kidding; his little sister really had grown up on him. He wasn't sure how he felt about that. He was proud of her, but felt a little at a loss, too. He hadn't realized it, but it seemed he'd liked being needed.

Then there was Logan Clark. Logan was obviously one of his best friends. And, of course, he was a good guy. Hardworking, loyal, kind. He was Amish, too.

But . . . that didn't mean he wasn't a man alone with his little sister. And, well, Tricia really was kind of pretty.

His mind spun. Then there was the fact that if he was realizing Trish wasn't a kid anymore, Logan was realizing that, too.

What if the blizzard continued? What if they were alone there for another day? And night? Hating the direction of his thoughts, he tried to shrug it off.

But again and again, the idea of the two of them getting far too close teased him.

Maybe he ought to try to do something more about it.

"Andy?" his mom called out. "What are you doing? I thought you were going to head down to the beach with us."

"I am. Go ahead and I'll meet you."

"What's keeping you?" Walking down the hall to where he was standing on the back patio, she frowned. "I know you have a life back in Walnut Creek, but I thought you were going to take some time off work."

"I am. This is personal. And I'm almost done."

Concern melted into interest. "Does it involve Kalie?"

He'd been dating Kalie off and on for the last four months. At the moment, they were firmly in the "off" category. Though he didn't like to share too much with his parents, Mom actually knew Kalie and loved her. She hadn't been shy about hinting that he and Kalie would make a great couple for the long term.

But since he was trying hard not to give away Tricia's secrets, he was almost thankful for his mother's Kalie obsession. "Sorry, Mom, but no. But, um, I was thinking that I should call her."

Her eyes lit up. "I think that's a fine idea. I'm sure she's been missing you."

He hoped his smile didn't look as strained as it felt. "I'll meet you and Dad in fifteen minutes."

"All right. All right," she said as she waved a hand. "I understand. No boy wants to talk to his girl with his mother lurking around. But tell her I said hello, okay?"

This was getting worse and worse. "Okay."

When he was alone again, Andy thumbed through his contacts, debating his options. He could trust Logan and Trish. He could remind himself how they were adults and any decision they made wasn't his business anyway.

Or . . . he could do what he'd always done and try to take care of her. And because some habits die hard, the decision was made.

Not all of the Eight had access to cell phones or landlines, of course. But even among the Amish, things were different than they used to be. Remembering that Harley had his own construction business and that the bishop had given him permission to use the phone for work, Logan decided he would call it.

Yes, he was completely taking advantage of the situation, but he couldn't help himself. One day he might not be able to help Trish as much as he could now. Until then, he was going to do what he could to make sure his little sister was as safe as possible.

Refusing to debate the pros and cons another moment, he pressed Send.

Two rings later, he picked up. "Harley here."

"Harley, it's Andy."

"Andy? Now, this is a surprise. I thought you were in Florida."

"I am. Look, I'm sorry to call you. I know your phone is just for business, but I think I need your help."

"What do you need?"

Briefly he filled him in about Tricia and Logan getting snowed in at the cabin. "So, you see why I'm concerned."

Harley started laughing. "*Nee,* I see why Tricia practically hung up on you. You are worrying too much, friend. And maybe thinking about things you shouldn't."

He felt his cheeks flush. "I know. But I can't help it. What do you think I should do?"

"Well, I think you should go swimming in the ocean and be thankful that you ain't stuck in the *shnay* like the rest of us are."

"That's it?" Be glad he wasn't stuck in the snow?

Harley chuckled again. "I'm just joshing ya. If I were you, I'd be doing the same thing. Worrying and fretting."

For some strange reason, that made him feel better. "Really?"

"*Jah.* To be sure. Logan is a good man, but the two of them alone for days? That ain't *gut.*"

Recalling Tricia's comment about beds, he groaned. "Any ideas about what I should do?"

Harley paused for a moment. "Nothing that you can do, *Englisch,* but I have an idea."

"And that is what?"

"I'll stop by and talk to Marie, John B., and Elizabeth Ann. Maybe the four of us can go out there to join them."

"How? Tricia said the weather's terrible."

"*Jah,* it is. It's a fair to bad *shtoahm,* and that's a fact," Harley agreed in his typical good humor. "But our Marie has a fancy new SUV. Maybe she'll like the idea of driving some of her Amish friends out to your cabin."

Just as Andy was nodding at that option, he said, "Do you think Logan's going to get mad when he finds out that I called you, too?"

"Of course not," Harley said so quickly that Andy knew he was lying. "But it don't matter anyhow. He'll get over it. Besides, we've all known each other far too long to get too upset about this. We've been through far worse. Ain't so?"

Harley was right. Ever since they'd all met at the Kurts' house, the eight of them had weathered lots of storms together. Some had been pretty intense, such as when John B.'s baby sister passed away. Others had just been normal problems, like when Katie had gotten

85

stung by a swarm of angry hornets. "You're right. Thanks."

"Go out and enjoy yourself, Andy. I'll reach out to Marie and whoever else I can find, and then we'll all go out and help take care of your *shveshtah.* It's a promise."

If Harley promised, then it would be done. "Thanks again," Andy replied, finally breathing easier. "Call me if you have a problem, though, okay?"

"To be sure. Bye, now."

After stuffing his phone in the pocket of his shorts, Andy slipped his sunglasses back over his eyes, hoping the shade would help to fade the headache that he couldn't seem to shake.

Then he started walking down the

pier to meet his parents and enjoy the beach. He was glad he'd called Harley. The guy was the most practical of the Eight. So steadfast, too.

And he'd been exactly right. Over the years, the eight of them had been through so much, and he feared they were destined to go through so much more.

Six

Four of the Clark kids were out in the front yard playing volleyball. The moment Andy and I came into view, Logan waved us over with a hand. "Andy, get over here! We need ya."

"My sister Tricia is here, too."

"I see her." Logan smiled more broadly. "Come join us, Tricia. Pick a side and don't hold back."

Because I didn't really have a choice, I started forward, but the whole time I was wishing I was anywhere else.

Tricia had been quiet ever since she'd spoken to Andy. Logan would even describe it as quieter than usual. She'd seemed especially shy and nervous the whole time he'd been here. At first, he'd thought it was because she was afraid, but he was beginning to think it had more to do with him than the situation.

He'd bided his time since she hung up. He'd made himself a peanut butter and jelly sandwich and sat at the small table while he ate it. He watched her walk around the cabin. Stare out of the window at the snow. Sip water.

And avoid meeting his eyes.

He was used to taking care of other people. That was what happened when one was born into a large family with lots of younger siblings. It was second nature to try to help someone in need, especially someone who was younger. But he wasn't sure if that was the best course of action. Andy was already bossy. She had her parents, who everyone knew never shied away from speaking their minds. She didn't need another guardian.

After another five minutes passed, he knew it was time to clear the air. All his silence was doing was making Tricia even more distant.

"Tricia, how about a sandwich,

too?"

She paused. "Hmm? Oh, no thanks, Logan. I'm fine."

"Are you sure? I haven't seen you eat anything since I've been here."

She ran her hands down her thighs. "Obviously I don't miss too many meals. I'll be fine."

Just as he felt himself watch those hands run down her legs, too, he snapped his head back up. "Why do you do that?"

She paused. "Do what?"

"Look for some kind of perceived flaw about yourself."

"It's not perceived, Logan. I'm not the skinniest girl in the world."

"You ain't the biggest *maydel,* either." When she looked a little shocked by his words — just as he was — he continued. "You must know you have a pleasing figure."

She walked closer. "Pleasing?"

Now he was absolutely wishing he had never said anything at all. As compliments went, it was sorely lacking. But since he'd hopped on this track, he nodded. *"Jah."*

Actually, Tricia's figure was far more than pleasing. By his estimation, she was all sweet curves and soft skin. She wasn't very tall, that was true. But he, for one, liked her figure. He knew a man didn't like worrying about if the woman he was with was too delicate. He didn't want to have to worry about hurting or bruising her if he held her too close or too tight.

Or, he supposed, if they were doing something far more intimate. Not that he should ever think about such things in regard to her.

Heat had bloomed in her cheeks. She pressed her palms to them. "I can't believe I'm blushing."

"I fear I'm blushing, too." Of course, his flush was unfortunately from thoughts that weren't vague at all. "I'm sorry. I don't know how to say how I think you look. I mean, this ain't my usual type of conversation, Tricia."

She giggled. "It's not mine, either."

"You know, I didn't ask. Did this man, this Emerson, did he hurt you?"

"Do you mean like did he hurt me beyond my feelings?"

"Jah."

"No. I mean, his words upset me, but he wasn't abusive or anything. They just made me self-conscious and cautious."

"So hurtful your grades fell."

She nodded slowly. "And since my grades have been pretty much the best thing I've had going for me lately, it's been really difficult."

"I've never cared about your grades, you know."

"You might just be the only one." Blowing out a burst of air, she shrugged. "Logan, now that I've calmed down a little, I've thought about my relationship with him. It's made me do a lot of thinking about the type of men I've been dating. So even though I've managed to get myself into another mess, I'm glad I stayed behind."

Logan leaned back in his chair. "What kind of men have you been dating?" he asked lightly, hoping she couldn't hear the jealousy in his voice.

"Men that are destined to become frogs."

"Frogs?"

Her eyes widened. "I'm sorry. Do you know that term? It has to do with a fairy tale. Something about a girl kissing a lot of frogs but then one of them turns into her own Prince Charming."

"I knew what you meant, Tricia. I haven't lived under a rock, you know."

"Sorry," she said, looking amused.

"Anyway, Emerson might have been a lot of things, but he definitely wasn't ever going to be my Prince Charming."

"Is that what you want? A prince?"

"Actually, no. I'm not in the market for a prince. Just a nice guy whom I can trust."

"Surely men like that aren't too hard to find."

She met his gaze before looking away. "You're right. I do know some guys who are like that."

"But?"

"But they, um, aren't for me."

What did that even mean? While he pondered that statement, all while cursing himself for even getting them into this conversation, she sat down at the table across from him.

"What about you? Do you have a girlfriend?"

"Nee."

"Why not?"

Because he'd been thinking too much about a certain brown-eyed girl he couldn't have. "I guess I haven't been ready."

She tore off a corner of his sandwich and popped it in her mouth. "Ready for what?"

He blinked, almost struck dumb. While Tricia had been fantasizing about frogs and princes, he'd been dreaming about marriage. "I'm speaking of marriage, Tricia," he said. "I'm not ready for marriage yet."

"Of course you aren't. I mean, Andy isn't ready for marriage, either. Can you imagine him in a committed relationship? He's a mess! Why, his girlfriend would kill him."

Her words were true, for sure. Andy was a convoluted, complicated mess. He, on the other hand, was not. His problem revolved around not wanting to get into a relationship when someone else was on his mind. "Maybe Andy and I aren't so different as one might imagine."

"I'm speaking of you courting, though. Isn't there a girl who has struck your fancy?"

"Not really." No one who was suitable, anyway. He liked being

Amish, and he couldn't imagine a woman like Tricia ever giving up her comforts in order to live his chosen lifestyle.

Feeling her gaze resting on him, he shifted. "I'm still putting in a lot of hours at the Walnut Creek Grande. Between the hotel and the farm, I don't have much extra time. I need to have at least a couple more thousand dollars to put away before I can buy a *haus,* anyway." Hoping to lighten the conversation, he winked. "I'll wait to go courting until I'm a good catch."

"You already are, Logan," she said softly. "Any woman is going to feel lucky to have you as hers."

"Blessed," he corrected automatically.

"Hmm?"

"Not lucky. Blessed, *jah*?"

Still staring at him intently, she nodded.

Right then and there, he knew he hadn't been imagining the pull between the two of them. And though it might be wrong and might never amount to anything, it didn't stop the reality of it. There was a pull there. Something close and tangible and deeper than just a physical attraction or a shared history together.

Against his will, he found himself scanning her face, reacquainting himself with the exact shade of her eyes, taking note of the spray of freckles across her cheekbones, thinking about her lips yet again.

Wondering why she looked so kiss-able.

Wondering why the Lord had decided that they'd needed this adventure. Wondering what he was supposed to learn from it.

Abruptly, he got to his feet. "You know what? We should stop sitting around and get the fire going again. Then we need to take stock and see if we can heat something up over the flames."

"I guess I'll go look in the kitchen again."

"I brought some things, too. Just in case we got into this situation."

"You thought we might?"

"I hoped and prayed that we wouldn't. But you know how that goes. Sometimes even the most fervent prayers go unanswered."

"I can't argue with that," she murmured.

Walking over to the fireplace, Logan sighed. It was starting to feel like every word each of them said was laced with a hidden meaning.

This adventure of theirs was going to wear him out . . . and they hadn't talked about what they were going to do when it was time to go to sleep.

SEVEN

I'd lived in Walnut Creek all my life, but while Andy had always felt at home among the Amish, I never had. I was always afraid I would say and do the wrong things. All that, of course, made joining that impromptu volleyball game even harder.

Several hours had passed since they'd talked to Andy. After the phone call, they'd made some popcorn over the fire, eaten more peanut butter and jelly sandwiches, and played cards. Now it was dark. They would have to get ready for bed, which made Tricia blush just thinking about it.

They'd already decided to both sleep on the floor in front of the fireplace. There really wasn't another option; the bedrooms were freezing.

When Logan offered to search the storage closet in the back of the second bedroom for sleeping bags, more flashlights, and batteries, Tricia opened cabinets that she'd already searched and sorted through the items in the refrigerator and freezer that she'd already memorized. She didn't care, though. She'd happily pretend to be rummaging through the whole house for another hour if it meant that she didn't have to look Logan directly in the eye again.

When was she ever going to learn? Logan Clark was not interested in her. Even if they weren't next-door neighbors, even if he weren't her brother's good friend, he didn't like her that way.

Though she knew she looked childish, she kept her back to him as he walked across the small space. She wasn't the best at hiding her feelings. Right at this moment? It was bordering on impossible.

"Ah, Tricia?"

She cleared her throat. "Yes?"

"I think it's starting to warm up a bit." She heard him shift uneasily. "I found some sleeping bags and other supplies, too. We can sort through them when I get back."

"From where?" she noticed he was putting on a thick coat and his hat again.

"I'm going to go outside."

She was facing the window. Even through the darkness, she could see that the wind was blowing so hard, it looked like the snow was falling sideways. Goodness, it couldn't be worse weather out. He must really want to take a moment away from her. "Are you sure that now is the best time to go out?"

"I need to check on the horses and get them bedded down for the night."

How had she forgotten them? "Oh! Of course. Do you need help?

I'll be glad to help you carry things, maybe get them more water?"

"Of course not. You stay in here where it's warm."

"I thank you for that, but I'm not helpless. I can even put on a coat and gloves to keep warm, just like you," she added sarcastically.

He sighed. "Trish —"

She cut him off. Trying to interject a happier tone, she said, "Sorry, I don't know why I say things like that sometimes. You go ahead. I've just been trying to figure out what can of soup would be best to heat up."

"Ah."

She realized then that she was staring at a cabinet full of flour and sugar and other baking products.

"I thought I might look to see what else we have, too."

"You know what? I completely forgot. When I arrived, I tossed my backpack on one of those chairs. There's a couple of things in it. Feel free to take out the food."

"I'll do that."

He edged toward the door. "Okay. Well, then. I'll be right back."

"Take your time. I'll be fine."

He didn't reply before walking out the door, a flashlight that he'd brought from home in his hand.

Thankful for the bright beam of light, she stood in front of the window and watched him slowly make his way to the shed, wincing as the snow seemed to swirl around him even harder with each step he took.

When he at last went inside, she breathed a sigh of relief and turned around, resting her head against the cabinet doors. Glad to have a few moments of privacy, she closed her eyes in frustration.

And in silent acknowledgment of what she couldn't deny.

Even though they were older and no doubt had little in common anymore, she still felt that same pull that she'd had back when she was ten years old and he'd smiled at her in his yard. Even though they hadn't had more than a few meaningful conversations over the last couple of years, that awareness that she felt around him was alive and well.

Flourishing, in fact.

What was she doing, acting like a little girl in the midst of her first crush? Hadn't she learned anything over the years? She really, really needed to get a handle on herself.

Walking to the table, she opened Logan's backpack. It was a faded army green and sported a well-known label from an outdoors company. Unable to help herself, she ran a hand over the worn fabric, thinking how the item fit him so well. Logan was Amish but not sheltered. Steadfast but not stuffy. Loyal to his traditions and values but not opposed to appreciating things outside the "typical" Amish world — such as the value of a well-made backpack.

Opening up the main compartment, she spied a metal ring of keys, a fresh shirt and pair of socks, three plastic containers of food that his mother had probably packed, and one package of Oreos.

Oreos! Amused, she sat down on one of the chairs and gazed at the extremely English treat. A stranger might have thought he'd brought the cookies for her, but she knew better.

Logan Clark had a really big sweet tooth.

Ten minutes later, the door blew open. "It's getting mighty cold out there, Trish. I bet the temperature's dropped another ten degrees."

"How are the horses?" Even that small burst of wind that had accompanied him through the door chilled her.

He shrugged as he pulled off his gloves and coat. "Not especially pleased, but they seem to be all right."

"I hope it's not too cold for them? I'd feel so bad if they got sick."

He chuckled. "You have such a soft heart, Tricia. They are sturdy horses, *jah*? They're used to pulling buggies in the rain and sleighs in the snow. They're dry and comfortable enough. They're disgruntled because they ain't home. They like their creature comforts."

"I guess I can relate. Though this cabin is cozy, it isn't home. I guess that's why I feel so out of sorts." It was the truth, just not the complete truth. But she hoped it was close enough to excuse her earlier panic attack.

Pulling out the chair across from her, he sat down. "You were out in the middle of nowhere with no electricity and no one to lean on. You shouldn't feel awkward about calling your *bruder* and askin' for help."

"It doesn't matter anyway. What's done is done." Pushing the package of cookies to the center of the table, she smiled. "Besides, nothing can be too bad if we have Oreos, right? I can't believe you brought these, Logan."

"It weren't anything."

She disagreed. "But still, you stopped by the store and picked them up. That was really nice of you."

"I didn't stop anywhere," he protested. "I had them on hand."

Opening the package's side, she pulled out two. "You know, it would be a shame if we didn't eat at least a couple."

He picked up one. "I was just thinking the same thing. I mean, we can't let them go to waste." With a wink, he popped one into his mouth.

The look of pure pleasure that lit his face made her laugh. "You are such a kid when it comes to treats, Logan Clark."

"I know. It's a fault of mine, for sure. I know I should feel badly about my need for sweet treats, but

I *canna* seem to help myself. I'm addicted."

After eating another three, she stood up. "Do you want anything else to eat?"

"*Nee*. I'm pretty tired, if you want to know the truth."

"Let's get the sleeping bags organized."

After closing the package, Tricia walked over to join him in the living room. Logan was standing beside the two sleeping bags, a stack of blankets, and a pile of pillows she'd taken out of one of the bedrooms while he'd been with the horses.

Earlier, when she'd placed everything in a haphazard pile, she was thinking only about warmth and comfort.

Now?

It seemed all she could think about was how intimate it felt to be sleeping in even the same room as him. She cleared her throat. "How would you like to organize every-thing?"

"It don't matter to me." He paused. "I'm guessing we should both be as close to the fire as pos-sible. It's gonna get even colder during the night."

Feeling a little silly that she was acting like such a child, she pulled out the red sleeping bag and set it down on the left side in front of the fire. Kneeling down, she loosened the cord around it. "I'll take the left side," she said unnecessarily. After all, where she had decided to be was obvious.

But if Logan thought she was being amusing, he didn't let it show. Instead, he came to her side, two thick blankets in his arms. "Let me help you."

"No, it's fine."

He ignored her. "The trick to sleeping on the ground, Trish, is a good padding." Kneeling next to her, he placed one blanket on the ground and then carefully set her sleeping bag on top of it. Then, as she watched, he unzipped the top of the bag a few inches, turned a corner down, and placed the other blanket on top of it all. Just as if she were a child.

"I don't need you to do this,

Logan. I'm not a little girl."

He popped his chin up and met her eyes. "Believe me, I know that."

She realized two things right then and there. The first was that Logan was just as affected by the suddenly intimate atmosphere as she was.

And second, no matter what happened between them during the rest of their lives, she would never be able to forget the heated, almost pained expression on Logan's face.

He looked exactly the way she was feeling in her heart.

EIGHT

"Are ya going to join us or not?" Sarah, Logan's younger sister, called out.

I didn't really want to. Even barefoot and wearing her pale-blue dress and white *kapp,* Sarah looked more athletic than I did in my shorts, T-shirt, and Keds.

But still, I hesitated. What if I was so terrible at volleyball that I made my team lose? Sarah didn't look like she'd take that in stride.

119

"Don't think so hard," Logan said with a smile. "It's just a game. Ain't so?"

As morning dawned and thin beams of sunlight crisscrossed the cabin's living room, Tricia groaned. Her eyes felt like sandpaper. Had either of them slept a wink? She wasn't sure. Even with logs burning brightly in the fireplace, the cabin had been freezing. Poor Logan had gotten up from his pallet on the floor almost hourly to tend to the logs. Every time she'd offered to help, he'd brushed it aside, whispering that she needed her rest.

Then there had been the constant noise. Outside, the wind had howled so loud that it seemed like a pack of wolves was circling the property. Gusts of wind had brushed some pine trees' branches against one of the cabin's walls and windows. Almost as soon as she got used to one noise, the wind would change direction and a clatter would erupt. For a while, she'd been expecting one of those branches to break off and fly through the glass.

But as distracting as the cold and the wind had been, neither of them held a candle to the most distract- ing thing of all — the fact that Logan Clark was lying down just to her right.

Barely three feet away.

She'd told Andy the truth. She

wasn't a sheltered child any longer. She'd spent the last two and a half years away in college and had experienced most things other college students did. She'd stayed out late and done more than a few activities that she should've thought twice about.

She'd slept on floors in her girlfriends' rooms and had studied for hours on couches in the library with other kids in her classes. She'd even spent the night with a group of men and women during a retreat for one of the campus charities. So it wasn't the fact that she was alone with a man that was disconcerting.

It was that she was alone with *him.* With Logan.

Everything that he did felt amplified. She'd heard every mumble or light snore. She'd been aware of every time he tossed and turned. She now knew what his face looked like when he was fast asleep and what his hair looked like first thing in the morning.

And what his cheeks looked like when they were scruffy and in need of a shave.

Yep, no matter how much she tried to not look at him, not notice every movement and faint mumble or grunt, she couldn't seem to hear anything else. All of her senses were firmly focused on him. She couldn't have pretended he wasn't sleeping next to her in the room if she'd tried.

The only saving grace was that

Logan had seemed just as aware of her. A new tension had sprung up between them, pulling so taut that she was tempted to stop pretending to sleep. The only reason she didn't say anything to him was because she couldn't think of anything to say.

Around two or three in the morning, Logan had gotten up and walked to the kitchen.

Unable to stop herself, she'd called out to him. "Are you all right?"

"Of course, Tricia," he replied, his voice sounding strained. "Just getting water."

"Oh."

"Do you want me to bring you a glass?"

Even half-asleep, he was so kind. "No. Thanks."

"Sorry, I didn't mean to wake you. Try to go to sleep, okay?"

" 'Kay." Though she'd been tempted to say something more, she didn't. She'd been too aware of him. Too tempted to look at him too long, just so she'd remember what he looked like in the middle of the night.

Which, of course, embarrassed her. He'd come to her rescue because his friend had asked him to, not because he particularly cared about her.

Feeling more despondent than ever, she'd turned onto her side and closed her eyes. In the distance, she heard the faucet go on. Heard a cabinet open and shut. Imagined he was staring out the kitchen window at the storm.

She'd fallen asleep imagining him standing there. So close but yet so far.

Now it was near nine in the morning and she was huddled in her sleeping bag, watching Logan sleep. Their roaring fire had dwindled to a slow burn, and the stockpile of wood in the holder was now empty. Because of that, the temperature had to have dropped to the low fifties.

She needed to go out and get more wood and bring it in but kept giving herself excuses, her latest being that all the movement would probably disturb Logan. She certainly didn't want to ruin his sleep.

Propping herself on her elbows, she glanced out the window on the other side of the room. It was still snowing; heavy, wet flakes swirled in the air and stuck to the glass.

Even from her position on the floor, it was obvious that there was no way they were going to be able to leave the cabin today.

That meant Logan was going to be stuck with her for another day and night, and the poor horses were going to have to stay in the shed. She didn't know much about horses, but she feared they were going to be worse off for this adventure. Especially since she knew they didn't have any food stored for them.

Just as she felt the burden of guilt weigh down her body again, she heard the roar of an approaching engine.

Ignoring the chilly air, she jumped to her feet and hurried to the window. In the distance, she saw the faint flash of headlights. Someone was at the far end of the drive.

Alarmed, she turned to her sleeping companion. "Logan, wake up!"

With a fierce inhale, he jerked to a sitting position. "What?"

"I just saw some headlights. I think someone's driving over to see us."

Rubbing his eyes, he blinked several times and then yawned. "Maybe it's a snowplow."

"A snowplow?"

"*Jah.* Do you get those out here?"

"I don't know. It seems doubtful, though." She peered out of the window again. "This isn't a snow-plow. Even from this distance, I can tell it's a truck." When the wind switched directions, lessening the snow for a few seconds, she got a better look. "I think it's a big SUV."

After stretching his arms, Logan walked to her side. Like her, he was wearing thick socks on his feet. However, while she had gotten up a few hours ago and quickly changed before hopping back in her makeshift bed, he was still wearing his clothes from yesterday, though they were all far more rumpled. She thought he looked like a teenager with his golden hair sticking up every which way.

After yawning again, he pressed a hand on the ledge and leaned against it. "Guess we're gonna get company, Trish."

"Who do you think it is?" Her mind spinning, she thought of the various possibilities. "Do you think it could it be the sheriff or something?" she asked, trying not to panic. "Maybe he is checking cabins to make sure we're okay."

"That would be nice if sheriffs did house calls like that, but I'm pretty sure this ain't him," he murmured as the approaching vehicle came into view.

"I bet you're right. I don't think many sheriffs drive big black Cadillac Escalades around in the snow."

"I *canna* think of anyone who does . . . well, maybe one," he murmured.

"Who?" She could hardly believe it. "Logan, are you telling me that you recognize this car?"

"Oh, *jah.*" After a second or two, he turned to her. "You know this vehicle, too, Tricia. Marie has arrived."

"Marie?" She tried to hide her dismay. While Tricia might have always felt comfortable around Logan Clark, she'd also always been extremely intimidated by Marie Hartman.

Marie was everything Tricia had never been. Thin and tall, popular, beautiful, and confident. Not only that, she'd been homecoming queen her senior year in high school. Andy had even been her escort on the football field.

Torn between being glad that the newcomer was a friend and feeling the burst of apprehension that she was going to be around Marie without Andy, she glanced at Logan again. "Do you really think that's Marie Hartman?"

He nodded. "Yep," he said as they watched the vehicle slowly roll to a stop next to the edge of a snowdrift about ten or twenty yards away.

Then, after honking twice, not one but three car doors opened.

Logan chuckled. "*Jah,* it's Marie all right. And, by the looks of things, it seems that she didn't come alone."

NINE

"Andy, you go over with Sarah, I've got Tricia here," Logan called out.

Andy didn't look all that happy. "Are you sure you want her?"

Logan smiled. "Oh, *jah.* Mighty sure."

Muttering under his breath, Andy walked over to Sarah's side. As he stomped away, Logan laughed. "Do you even know how to play volleyball, Trish?"

I felt my cheeks flush as I nodded. The moment he turned away, I immediately started hoping and praying that I wasn't about to make a fool of myself.

Seeing the look of trepidation on Tricia's face, Logan was tempted to give her a hug. Anything to reassure her that she wasn't the only one to feel disappointed that they weren't alone anymore.

All the progress that the two of them had made in their relationship was about to evaporate. He hated that.

"Don't look so worried. Marie's

great. I'm sure whoever is here is going to be a friend, too," he said as he walked to the kitchen sink and splashed some cold water on his face. It was bitter cold, but it served to push the last of the sleep off his face.

"Did you know they were coming?" she asked as she walked over to the hooks by the door and pulled on her coat.

"Nope. I didn't talk to your *bruder* yesterday, you did." As he stuffed his feet into his boots, he said, "Did Andy give you any indication that he was going to call around?"

"No. He didn't sound all that happy that the two of us were going to be living here alone, but I let him know he was being ridiculous.

I don't know what he thought we'd be doing."

An image of him pulling her into his arms and breaking down all the barriers that stood between them flashed into Logan's brain before he could push it away. Fearing that she could read his mind, he waved a hand. "You know Andy. He's always imagining something is going on that isn't."

"But nothing has been going on. I mean, not besides the two of us doing just fine."

"It don't really matter anyway." Hoping to sound happier than he was, he lightened his tone. "Just think, in a couple of hours, you'll be back at your house, warm and comfortable. This whole thing will be over. Let's go meet them."

Tricia smiled faintly before opening the door and waving for him to go first.

He did, but only because he wanted to act as a buffer between her and everyone who was arriving.

Almost another foot of snow had fallen during the night. Their boots sank into it while more floated around their faces and necks. Beside him, he heard Tricia take a fortifying breath.

He was just about to give her a small word of encouragement, when he heard his name.

"Logan!" Elizabeth Ann called as she climbed out of the back seat. "You are a sight for sore eyes."

He barely had time to hold his

hands out before she tumbled into his arms for a hug. "You are acting like Tricia and I have been lost in the wilderness instead of stuck in a cabin in the woods."

"You might as well have been that way," Harley said as he came around and clapped him on the back. "Getting here was pretty nerve-racking, I'll tell you that."

"Uh-oh. What happened?"

"You name it," Marie said. "Traffic, car accidents, and unplowed roads. What usually takes about an hour and a half took almost three."

Elizabeth Ann nodded. "It was really bad."

"We were going to come out last night, but my parents heard that the weather was worse. We decided to head out early this morning," Marie continued as she followed Tricia and Elizabeth into the cabin.

"At least you're here now," Logan said as he closed the door behind him and Harley. "Now, please tell me you brought us some coffee."

Harley groaned. "That's all you have to say?"

Grinning, Logan inclined his head. "Very well. *Danke* for coming here," he said politely. "Do you happen to have any hot coffee with you? Any at all?"

Elizabeth looked at their pair of sleeping bags still littering the living room floor. "Looks like you've been having a slumber party."

"You can see that we've been cold and sleeping by the fire," Logan said, feeling more than a little irritated with the knowing looks his friends were sending one another.

"It hasn't been that bad," Tricia protested.

No, it had actually been really nice. Probably too nice. Hating that his mind was going back to Tricia again, Logan tried to pretend that he was relieved by their arrival. "Even though I'm going to have to stay behind and care for Priscilla and Pet, I'm relieved that you'll be able to get Tricia back home. Andy's going to be happy about that."

The three of them exchanged looks again. "What's going on?" he asked slowly.

"Well," Marie began, "I'm not real sure if things are going to work like that."

"I don't understand," Tricia said.

Harley softened his voice. "Trish, what Marie's trying to tell ya is that we're going to have to wait at least a day to take you anywhere."

"Why?" Logan asked. "Are the roads still really that bad?"

"They really are," Marie replied. Shivering a bit, she added, "Growing up in Walnut Creek, I'm fairly used to driving in snow. Now that I've been in Cleveland for two years, I've driven home in some pretty nasty weather, too. But this short trip getting here was *bad.* I don't know if I've ever attempted to drive through worse."

Tricia covered her mouth with a hand. "I'm so sorry that you had to go through all of that because my brother called you."

"Don't go putting that burden on your shoulders," Elizabeth Ann said. "We wanted to be here and we're glad we could help. But honestly, it's like the snowplows didn't leave their garages today."

"Right as we pulled off the highway, we heard a new weather alert. They just upped the weather advisory to a Level Three. No one is supposed to be on the roads right now," Harley said. "Another storm's on its way."

"Another one?" Tricia said as she walked to the windows. Already at least a foot of snow covered everything in sight. "I can't believe this."

Logan noticed the way her shoulders had slumped. It was obvious that she was feeling as though her bad choice to come to the cabin had steamrolled into a minor disaster. He didn't feel that way, and he knew the others didn't, either . . . but he couldn't deny that he would have probably felt the same way. "So you all are going to be spending the night tonight," he murmured. "Maybe even tomorrow night, too."

"Yup," Harley said with a shrug. "I'm telling ya, Logan, I knew it was bad, but it seems to have taken everyone by surprise. We listened to the weather reports most of the way here. Some kind of terrible freak storm is brewing over the Great Lakes and fixing to dump snow along northern Ohio."

Elizabeth Ann nodded. "They're expecting another foot of snow."

Tricia groaned.

"Luckily for you, we brought a bale of hay, grain, and some blankets for the horses, too," Harley said.

"Harley had it all ready to go when I picked him up," Marie explained.

"Then we decided to run to the Walmart and grab a bunch more things for all of us."

"Including a carafe of hot coffee, Logan," Marie added with a grin.

Logan closed his eyes. "Bless you."

Harley rolled his eyes. "You should be more grateful that I'm feeding your *gauls.*"

"I am, but I need some *kaffi* in a bad way."

Marie playfully nudged him with her shoulder. "Don't say I never get you anything."

"I promise, I'll never say that again," he teased.

Elizabeth Ann pointed to the door. "Come on, everybody," she said in her typical practical manner. "We need to stop talking and unload Marie's vehicle and get organized. There's a ton to put away."

Looking at the lot of them, Logan grinned. "Just how much did you all bring?"

"About as much as you might think Marie could pack in two

hours," E. A. said.

"Oh, my," Trish murmured.

"*Jah.* It's stuffed to the gills," Harley said. "But that's all right, ain't so? That means you two will have plenty of time to tell us all about what you've been doing in this here cabin to make the time go by faster. We've had quite a *gut* time guessing."

Feeling Tricia tense up next to him, Logan yearned to clasp her hand and remind her that she was with friends. Harley especially loved to tease and joke, but he would never intentionally hurt or embarrass her.

Tricia had to know that she was safe. That there was nothing she could say that would be taken the wrong way or twisted and repeated to either her parents or even Andy.

That was the beauty of the Eight, and the depth of their friendship. Surely she understood?

But when he turned to her with a wink, he noticed Tricia had turned pale.

He winced as he realized something he should've known a long time ago. She didn't see that at all.

TEN

My first attempt at serving was worse than bad. The volleyball kind of flew up in the air, then sailed straight back down, nearly hitting Logan's foot.

"I'm fairly sure the goal is to hit the ball over the net, Trish," he murmured.

His sister Sarah just glared.

Tricia had known Marie Hartman ever since they were little girls and

Andy had brought her over to play one day. Even when Marie was younger, she'd always reminded Tricia of one of those fancy American Girl dolls her grandmother had given her for Christmas. It was probably a good comparison even now. Marie positively embodied class — probably because her parents, who were richer than sin, had done things like take her to London and Paris on vacation.

She was polished and confident and never seemed to ever have the social mishaps that had marked Tricia's life.

Back in high school, Marie had also been really popular, more than Andy had been, and even Tricia realized that pretty much everyone in their school had liked her brother.

All of that would have been enough to make Tricia feel like the awkward teenage girl that she'd been in high school. However, there was something more about Marie that had been almost even harder to take.

She was nice. Really nice. So much so that Tricia had never known what to say to her whenever their paths crossed.

Now, all these years later?

It seemed things hadn't really changed. Marie was wearing skinny jeans, a beautiful pair of fuzzy designer boots, and a light-green sweater that was almost the same shade as her eyes. She'd put her long hair in a complicated variation of a French braid, and it hung down the middle of her back.

After sleeping on the floor and barely even brushing her hair? Tricia felt more than frumpy by her side.

They were alone in the cabin. Marie had offered to help Tricia clean up the blankets and sleeping bags while Harley and E. A. went out to the shed with Logan.

"So, how have things been going with just the two of you here?" Marie asked.

"They've been fine."

Looking like she was hiding a secret, Marie smiled. "I bet."

Feeling like those two words were meant to convey something personal, Tricia felt even more flustered. "What do you mean by that?"

"Nothing, other than it's been pretty obvious that there's something special between the two of you."

"There isn't," Tricia said quickly. "I mean, not beyond the fact that he drove his sleigh out here in the snow for my brother."

"For Andy?"

"Well, yeah. I get it. All of you eight are so close. I know each of you would do anything to help my brother out."

"You really think that, don't you?"

"It's true. I mean, you drove here in a bear of a storm to help Logan because Andy called."

"I came out here for you, too."

Now Tricia sounded whiny and ungrateful. "I'm sorry. This isn't coming out like I wanted it to."

Marie pushed a chunk of golden hair off her shoulders. "No, I'm the one who needs to apologize. Here you've been living in the dark and the cold, and practically the first thing I do is tease you about Logan. That was pretty mean."

Tricia had kind of thought so, too. "I'm glad you came here, but I'm sorry you're going to be stuck tonight."

She laughed. "If I was with other people, I'd feel worse. But being here, out in the snow, with no way to get on the computer and no way to get home? I'm thinking it's kind of fun, if you want to know the truth."

"I guess everyone has their own idea of fun."

"I just mean that I'm sick of working in that bank. It's so busy, and there's so much stress. I needed a break, and this is giving me one."

"I had forgotten that you worked up in Cleveland. It's really that bad?"

"No." She pursed her lips. "The work is demanding, but I'm pretty good at it, you know? I've gotten two raises and a bonus. It shouldn't make a difference, but being able to pay my rent without worrying and being able to go out to dinner a couple of times a month makes everything seem better."

"I bet."

"But there's more. Tricia, when I moved to Cleveland, I went for a variety of reasons. I wanted to try so hard to find a new identity. I wanted people to get to know me based on my merits. By what they saw and how I worked, not by what they thought they already knew about me." She wrinkled her nose. "Does that make sense?"

"More than you realize." After all, hadn't she gone to Bowling Green specifically because Andy had gone to Ohio University? She had been desperate to attain her own identity. It was only recently that she'd realized her family and her relationship with her brother were part of her identity.

"All that is why I think I'm going to change offices and move home. I proved myself, but I think I lost part of me at the same time. I want that back."

"I didn't think there were any major banks in Walnut Creek."

"There aren't, but there's an office of Champion Bank in New Philadelphia. That's one of the reasons I was in town when Andy called. I had an interview there with the branch manager yesterday morning."

New Philly was close. Only a ten-minute drive on the highway. It was also nice enough, but it was still really small. Definitely a long ways away from working in downtown Cleveland. "There isn't much there, is there?"

"Nope." Looking strangely pleased, Marie shook her head. "There's not much at all. It's going to mean a pay cut, too. But on the flip side, I also won't be expected to work sixty hours a week."

"I can see how that would be a plus."

"Exactly." Propping a hand on her hip, she looked around. "Let's go unpack the food we brought and see if we can make soup or something over the fire."

"I can't believe you guys brought all of these supplies."

"I wouldn't have even thought about it, but Harley's neighbor told him that another storm was coming and we should be prepared for anything. After we picked up Elizabeth Ann, we headed straight to the supercenter and stocked up."

They'd come to see her and Logan even knowing they'd probably get stuck. "I hope I would have done this for someone else. I'm not sure, though."

Marie waved a hand, effectively brushing off her comment. "Of course you would have. You'd do it for Andy, right?"

"Well, yes." But he was her brother. "I just meant —"

Marie cut her off. "Don't worry about it, Tricia. It's not a contest or anything. It's just life."

Tricia liked that way of thinking. It made a lot of sense. Yes, absolutely. Everything that had been happening with Emerson and school and the storm . . . it was just life.

Life was messy and complicated, and not always going according to plan.

There was something to say for that.

"Hey, Trish?"

"Yes?"

For the first time since her arrival, Marie looked tentative. "Look, I know this is none of my business, but you do know that Logan already joined his church, right? He's been baptized. He's not going to stop being Amish."

"I realize that."

"So —"

"I'm well aware that we don't

have a future."

Marie looked away. "I'm sorry."

She lifted one shoulder. "Don't be. You . . . well, you are right. Life is messy and complicated. Especially when it comes to relationships."

A new line of worry creased Marie's perfect brow. "I hate to say it, but I think you're right. Relationships of all kinds are hard." Lowering her voice, she continued. "Sometimes they're so hard, it makes a person wonder why they even try."

Before Tricia could figure out how to respond to that, Marie turned to face her again. "Sometimes I think that it's a wonder any of us ever try to get involved with other people at all."

ELEVEN

And so it continued. Sarah and Andy played so well together that one would have thought they had dreams of turning professional.

Me and Logan? It was more like Logan was playing volleyball and I was trying to stay out of his way.

"What do you think Andy is going to say about you keeping company with his little sister?" Harley said as soon as Elizabeth Ann had left them to go into the house.

Logan and Harley had decided to take Pet and Priss for a brief walk in the snowy field by the cabin. Usually, Logan would have chosen to keep the horses inside, but they weren't in the best situation and their stalls weren't especially roomy. With the storm on the way, he wanted to give them some time to stretch their legs.

Glad that he'd put his gloves back on, he and Harley each took a horse and walked with it outside.

"Harley, I'm not sure what you want me to say to that. You know Andy called and asked me to go get Tricia."

"*Jah.* He called you to get Tricia. Not sleep in a cabin next to her."

"We couldn't leave. There's no

way it would have been safe for either Tricia or Pet and Priss."

"You know I ain't talking about the horses."

Now Logan was getting irritated. "You would've done the same thing, Harley. There's no heat. I wasn't going to make her sleep in one of the bedrooms by herself. And I'm a good friend, but not good enough to volunteer to freeze in one of them all for propriety."

"Protest all you want, but I still think that he ain't going to be happy with you."

"We haven't done anything. It's Tricia."

Harley laughed. "Exactly. You've liked Andy's little *shveshtah* for years . . . and she's always had a crush on you."

"If you think all that, then you'll be pleased to learn that she and I contained ourselves and didn't do anything."

"Ah."

"You also know that I got baptized the same year you did. There's no chance that Trish and I can have a future. I'm not jumping the fence."

"I remember you got baptized. That happened about four months after me, right?"

"Jah."

"So only John B. hasn't. I wonder why."

"John B. is confused about his life," Logan said. "He works at that *Englisch* company and has always liked modern things. I think he's been straddling two worlds for quite some time, even though his parents have no idea about that."

"Mine would be shocked."

"Mine would, too, but that doesn't matter. That isn't me."

Harley nodded slowly. "I guess you do have a point about John." They went to the edge of the field, encouraged the horses to turn, and then released them.

Usually, Pet and Priss would have enjoyed the freedom and run around a little bit. However, the horses just looked annoyed by the cold, snowy day. Pet blew out a burst of impatient air and pawed the ground.

Logan chuckled. "I hear ya, Pet.

We're heading back now."

As they started walking, he glanced back at Harley. "Look, I know you are only asking because you care, but I would never disrespect Tricia or Andy. And I don't think Tricia would, either. She's a nice girl."

"I've always liked her. And, as odd as it sounds, I've even been able to see you two together. Do you know what I mean?"

Logan wanted to say no. To share that he'd learned a long time ago that it didn't do anyone any good to start thinking about things that could never be.

But he didn't want to lie. And that was the hardest part to admit to himself. Because he could see that, too.

"I know what you mean." He liked being around her. He liked how they complemented each other and that being with her was so easy.

"Maybe she'd want to . . ." His voice drifted off.

Logan was grateful for that small favor. Tricia was a lot of things, but a girl contemplating becoming Amish? No, that wasn't her, not at all.

Ignoring the sudden burst of sadness that ran through him, he opened the shed's door. "Let's get the horses settled in their stalls."

They worked for the next twenty minutes, easing them inside, giving them fresh grain and hay. Breaking ice from the trough outside and getting the horses fresh water. Finally, they fastened the horse blankets onto the two of them. Neither horse shied away from the weight, seeming to enjoy the added comfort.

"*Danke* for bringing these for Pet and Priss. It was kind of you."

"It wasn't anything. Glad to do it." As they started back to the cabin, Harley smiled at him. "After all, that's what friends are for, ain't so?"

Fighting the lump that had formed in his throat, Logan nodded.

TWELVE

But then it happened. Sarah served, the ball sailed right toward me, and I folded my hands together. Then, wonder of wonders, I bumped it right back over the net. Since neither Sarah nor Andy was ready, we got a point.

Suddenly, the game was tied. "Look at you, Trish!" Logan exclaimed.

Maybe I was starting to look like

a volleyball player? I don't know. I couldn't see much past how perfect his smile was.

Somehow, even though the snowstorm was still raging outside, their newcomers had injected a party atmosphere into the cabin. Tricia could hardly believe how different she felt compared to just twenty-four hours earlier.

Then, she'd felt entirely alone in the world, and the lack of electricity had only intensified those feelings. It had taken everything she had to simply call her brother for help.

Later, when Logan joined her, she'd felt comforted, but had also fought an underlying tension brewing between them.

Logan symbolized so many things that she shouldn't want and couldn't have. She'd vacillated between being grateful for his presence and wishing he'd never come. She'd felt almost like a child again, torn between wanting a toy she couldn't have and realizing that it was always going to be out of her reach.

Now? With four of the Eight in the midst? Even in the dark, their laughter and warmth illuminated the room.

After they'd unloaded Marie's vehicle and put all the dry goods on the table, Tricia was amazed. It seemed like they'd intended to stay for a week instead of just one night.

Marie had laughed when she saw Tricia's incredulous expression. "You're going to have to get used to my tendency to pack everything but the kitchen sink, Trish. I'm willing to change a lot of things about myself but not that."

Tricia had grinned and, inside, felt a new warmth flow through her. Marie was talking as if they were now friends and would be spending time together again soon.

Later, after Harley and Logan got back from taking care of the horses, it became a game of sorts to make the best meal without electricity.

They'd done a good job of it, too. Harley, Logan, and Elizabeth Ann made a stew in a large cast-iron pot on the fire. Later, Tricia and Marie

found some old coat hangers, un-
twisted them, and passed out
marshmallows. True to the Eight,
they'd all started joking about who
could do the best job of roasting
the confection before mashing it
between two graham crackers and
a piece of chocolate.

Now the five of them were
wrapped up in blankets, layers of
clothes, and thick socks and sitting
in a semicircle, almost silently
watching the flames. The fire's glow
made the large room seem cozier
and more intimate.

Marie sighed. "It's a shame that
we have to have Andy call us for
help in order to get together. We
should do things like this more often."

Elizabeth Ann, her strawberry blonde hair glowing almost pink in the firelight, wrinkled her nose. "I don't know why we don't. I guess we all get too busy with our 'important' things."

Logan, who'd managed to heat up a kettle of water over the fire and then brew a cup of coffee in Tricia's mother's French press, set his mug down and stretched out his legs. "You know why we don't do it, E. A. It's because we've always counted on Andy to do the planning."

Elizabeth nodded. "This is true." She smiled at Tricia. "And here, even from Florida, your *bruder*'s gone and done it again. We're having an impromptu slumber party, something that hasn't happened in years. I wish he was here. He'd love it."

"I'm grateful that Andy called you all, and I know he'd love being here, but I can't believe he's really been that instrumental in getting all of you together over the years," Tricia said. "Surely you all meet every now and then without his prodding?"

"You're right, some of us do get together from time to time," Elizabeth Ann said. "But it's not the same." Glancing at Marie, she shrugged. "I don't know why."

Harley chuckled. "Tricia, you might be younger than us, but you're no fool. You know as well as we do that your *bruder* likes to be in charge."

"Yes, but I thought that was just his bossy nature. I mean, he loves to tell everyone what to do."

"There are some people who are simply *gut* at making plans," Logan said. "Andy is one of them. I can reach out to everyone and say hello, but I never come up with the ideas and encourage everyone to drop what they're doing to make it happen."

Marie smiled, her white teeth practically glowing in the darkened room. "He sure got me going last night. I wasn't on the phone with him five minutes before I was pulling out a suitcase from under my bed."

"You mean *suitcases,* plural,"

Harley teased. "I've never known a woman who needed so many things for every little thing she does."

"You seemed to enjoy those s'mores, Harley."

He winked at Tricia. "I suppose I did at that."

Logan stretched out his legs. "Well, I for one am glad you all came. I tried to be of help to Tricia, but all that happened is I put my horses in her shed and helped her eat peanut butter and jelly sandwiches."

"You know you did more than that," Tricia protested. "You brought me Oreos, too."

"You and your Oreos, Logan," Harley murmured.

"Hey, they make everything better!"

Smiling at him, Tricia continued. "I'm not going to lie. I was really scared until Logan showed up."

"I'm glad I got here yesterday," Logan murmured. "I don't like to think of you ever being scared and alone."

Elizabeth Ann tucked her legs under her dress as she turned to her. "Tricia, I know we probably aren't supposed to ask, but why did you come up here in the first place?"

Logan's face turned serious. "E. A. . . ."

"No, Elizabeth Ann's right to wonder," Tricia protested. "I think I owe all of you an explanation for my behavior."

"You actually don't," Logan said.

E. A. bit her bottom lip. "If you don't want to talk about it, we don't have to. You know I have a bad habit of being too blunt."

Tricia looked at all four faces staring back at her, each person waiting for her to say something to explain her situation. Even, she realized with a start, Logan.

"I don't know how much you know about what I've been doing. Andy has probably told you that I'm a junior at Bowling Green."

"He's told us you've made the dean's list every semester in some kind of mathematics," Harley said. "You're quite the scholar."

That praise embarrassed her. "I'm good at numbers. I'm about two-thirds of the way to earning a degree in applied mathematics."

Marie smiled at her. "I majored in accounting. I did fine, but I was definitely in the middle of the road, as far as grades go. Getting on the dean's list is commendable."

"We're all really proud of you," Elizabeth Ann said. "Andy especially."

"Thank you, but I don't know if I deserve so much praise. School has always been easy for me." Feeling like she was laying herself bare, she said, "Unfortunately, it's everything else that is so hard. I haven't had a very good time there. I haven't had a lot of luck making friends."

"Not even in your math classes?" Elizabeth Ann asked.

"That's the thing. A lot of the math nerds like me are real good with numbers but not necessarily with other people. And the ones who do make an effort?" She shuddered, just thinking about some of the conversations. "They're either really awkward or they revolve around school and math and future jobs. That's not their fault, though. It's mine."

"So that's why you came up here? Because you were lonely?" Marie asked.

Realizing how odd that would be, Tricia shook her head. "No. I did end up making two good girlfriends. I thought we were close, but then I started seeing Emerson."

"Let me guess, one of your friends

didn't like that one bit?"

Tricia shook her head. "I was such a mess. I thought Jen and Emerson were literally just friends. You know, like all of you. But it turns out that Jen thought they were a true couple. So when I went out with him, she got mad and refused to talk to me. I felt so bad and alone, I ended up seeing Emerson longer than I should have. Then we got in a fight and I told him that we were done."

"And that didn't go over real well?"

Remembering how ugly it had gotten, she said, "Your guess is right. He said some hurtful things that I can't seem to stop thinking about."

"You need to ignore what he said and try to forget about it," Marie said. "Trust me, everyone says things they don't mean when they're hurting."

"I would've brushed off his remarks if I thought they were all lies. But the more I thought about it, the more I began to realize he might have been right."

"What did he say?" Marie asked.

She really didn't want to share it. But so far, keeping it all to herself hadn't done any good. All she kept doing was trying to hide from herself. Taking a deep breath, she said, "He said I held everything in. That the problem wasn't the math students or the school or even our breakup. It was me. I didn't know how to have relationships."

Harley asked, breaking his silence, "Why would you think that would be true?"

"Why wouldn't it be?" Feeling awkward and frustrated, Tricia waved a hand. "I mean, look at what's happened."

"We're all hanging out at your family's cabin and eating too much?" Logan asked.

"No. Of course not. I mean, I get in trouble . . . who do I call? My brother. Why don't I have a large circle of friends like he does?"

"Because you don't need one," Logan said.

She gaped at him. "Of course I do."

"Nee," he said, shaking his head.

"You are misunderstanding me. Tricia, I'm not saying you don't need friends. I'm saying that you don't need *another* circle of friends because you have us."

His words were sweet but not exactly accurate. "That's kind of you to say, but I can't help but think about when we were all little. Logan has little sisters, I went to school with Marie's younger brother. How come I didn't click with anyone like Andy did?" She held up a hand. "And that's a rhetorical question. I don't think there's a real answer there."

When the whole group stayed silent, Tricia was tempted to get up and leave the room. She would rather spend the night in one of the freezing bedrooms than hear them say that she was exactly right.

That there really was something wrong with her.

Thirteen

Ten minutes later, Logan spiked the ball, Sarah missed it, and we won.

We won!

I was so excited, I turned to Logan and gave a little squeal. He responded by picking me up and twirling me in a circle.

Logan would have given each of his friends five bucks if he thought there was somewhere else they could go. Tricia was obviously in pain, just as it was obvious that she was finally revealing something that she'd been thinking about for a very long time.

Surely she wouldn't want all of them staring at her while she attempted to refocus and regain her composure?

But then, just as suddenly, he realized that she had chosen to bare her soul to all of them, not just him. There had to be a reason she'd chosen to do so at this time and this place. Either she had made this decision on her own, or God was working through them, knowing she was going to need all of their support in order to help her overcome her fears.

As the seconds passed, each one feeling like an eternity as the tense silence continued, Logan shared a glance with three of his best friends in the world.

Harley looked as closed as ever, but there was stark pain in his eyes, reminding Logan that Tricia wasn't the only person in the room who had endured doubts and hardships. Beside Harley, Elizabeth Ann and Marie were reflecting his same thoughts, each in her own way. Elizabeth, who'd always worn her heart on her sleeve, had tears in her eyes. And Marie looked like she was impatiently waiting on Logan to do something before she took the reins and ran to Tricia's side.

There was also something else

lurking among them all, and that was the belief not only that he needed to help Tricia, but that he was more than capable of doing it.

Just as Tricia stood to go, he heard her breath hitch, and he stepped close and reached for both of her hands. Right then and there, he knew. He knew what he needed to do.

Maybe he would have done something differently if they'd been alone. Maybe he might have even pulled her into his arms and kissed her. Or whispered gently how worthy she was and how there was nothing wrong with her.

But they weren't alone, and everything inside of him shouted that that wasn't what she needed.

Feeling empowered, he squeezed her hands and said, "Tricia, you must stop this."

Looking stung, she tried to pull away. He simply held on tighter. *"Nee,"* he said, emphasizing his motion. "I'm not going to let you run. I'm not going to let you do this to yourself, or to any of us."

"You?" Temper flared in her eyes. "Logan —"

"*Nee.* You listen to me. There is *nothing* wrong with you. There is nothing wrong with your ability to make friends. All of us came here to help you, not simply because we owed Andy a favor."

Behind them, Logan heard the others get to their feet as well. He knew they were ready to lend Tricia their support. For a moment, he was certain that Tricia realized that, too.

But she still looked doubtful.

"It's true," he said. "Look at me, Tricia. Do you really think I'm so weak that I would only do something because Andy asked me to?"

"You know that wasn't what I meant." Looking more upset, she darted a glance at the others in the room. "Look, can we all just forget what I said? Obviously I'm tired and not thinking clearly."

Marie stepped closer. "I bet you are tired. If I were you, I'd be exhausted, but I have to agree with Logan. We like you, Tricia. We like you for you, not just because you are Andy's sister. And let me tell you something else. As much as I love your brother, I have no desire for the world to be populated with more than one Andy Warner."

"None of us want that," Harley said. "I've probably spent half of my life fighting the urge to tell him to stop attempting to manage me."

"What about the second half?" E. A. asked.

"That's easy. I fight the urge to tell him that he's right."

Harley's comment broke the tension. They all started laughing, which made Logan finally release Tricia's hands.

She pressed them to her face and breathed in deep. When she dropped them, she looked calmer and more confident. "Thank you all for saying those things. It's really sweet of you. I'm just sorry that I brought it up in the first place."

"I'm not." Elizabeth Ann looked at all of them. "I'm realizing now that the four of us might have needed to have this conversation as much as you did. We've known each other a long time. And though there are eight of us, we've each managed to play a role in the group. Some of us are more protective, others are more patient." Smiling at Marie, she said, "Some of us are just too much."

"Hey!" Marie said. "You always said you loved me anyway."

E. A. grinned. "I do, but that's still the truth."

"What about you, E. A.?" Logan

asked.

"Me? Oh, that's easy. I'm guilty of being too supportive."

"I don't think anyone can be that way."

"Then you would be wrong. It's easier to keep one's mouth shut and tell a person what they want to hear, to make them feel good. It's a whole other thing to say and do the right thing."

"E. A."

"Harley, stop. You know I'm right." Turning back to Trish, she said, "Therefore, because you've inspired me, I'm going to push myself a bit and attempt to tell you what I think you need to hear." She bit her lip. "That is, if you don't mind?"

Tricia shook her head. "I don't mind."

"Here goes. Tricia, I've lived most of my life having my family and being part of the Eight. I'm grateful for everyone. I've depended on them, too. But if I had to move, I can tell you for certain that I wouldn't need a big group of boys and girls to have my back. Sometimes I think all a person needs is just one good friend to be by their side. Stop comparing yourself to other people. Stop doubting yourself and looking for flaws in order to prove that your doubts are correct. Instead, concentrate on the gifts that the Lord gave you."

Marie raised her eyebrows. "Wow, E. A."

"I know." Tilting up her chin, she said, "I'm right pleased with myself."

"I'm proud of you," Logan said. Casting a sideways glance at Tricia, he murmured, "Feel better?"

"Yes."

"Gut," Harley said. "Now, I suggest we clean up as best we can and get to sleep. You lazy birds probably slept in until seven or something. I, on the other hand, was up at five. I want to go to sleep."

Bending down to pick up the package of chocolate bars and the box of graham crackers, Marie sniffed. "Looks like you, too, have some hidden traits that we haven't seen coming. You sure are bossy all of a sudden."

"I've always been bossy, you just never chose to listen to me, Queen."

She gasped. "Harley, I can't believe you called me that."

"Why? You do have a crown."

"Well, I didn't bring it with me this time. But next time we're together, I'll be sure to slip it on and tell you what to do."

"I'm looking forward to it."

As they continued to bicker, Logan wrapped an arm around Tricia's shoulders. "Better?" he whispered.

"Better."

Gut. Then, before he could stop himself, he kissed her cheek.

When she smiled and blushed, he dropped his hand and turned away.

But not before realizing that some-thing had changed between them again.

He couldn't fight it anymore. He was falling in love with Tricia War-ner.

Fourteen

Logan released me almost immediately, but the damage had already been done. I was now certain that no other boy would ever be as perfect as Logan Clark, at least no other boy to me.

It turns out that I wasn't wrong.

A loud tap and a scrape against the window above her head woke Tricia up in the middle of the night. Inhaling sharply, she propped herself on her elbows and turned to the window, half expecting to see someone lurking on the other side.

But it was only a tree branch.

The wind had picked up overnight. By the sound of it, it had to be blowing gusts of thirty or forty miles an hour. They were shaking the limbs of the trees and seemed to be creating a harsh rattle between the planks in the cabin.

Sitting up straighter, she realized that the strong winds had blown the last remnants of the storm from of the vicinity. For the first time since she'd arrived, she could see stars in the sky and the moon's glow. Maybe this crazy trip was nearing its end.

Just as she gave thanks for that, she heard Harley's light snores from across the room. Which re-minded her that she wasn't alone at all.

Instead, she was now surrounded by two women and two men, all who had become her friends.

She turned her head, letting her attention linger on each of the other people in the room. Elizabeth Ann, with her sweet kindness. Har-ley, so quiet and steadfast. Marie, the pretty girl who was turning out to be so much more than Tricia re-alized.

And Logan. Her brother's friend whom she'd always tried so hard to not think about. But now? It seemed he was the man who was destined to be her future.

Though she'd thought it before,

she shook her head in wonder again. It turned out that her parents' favorite saying wasn't really a cliché after all. The Lord really did work in mysterious ways. Never would she have guessed that one desperate, unhappy choice would result in so many blessings.

She'd been reminded about her brother's love by the way he'd unabashedly called his friends and asked them to drop everything for her. She'd learned that she was stronger than she'd thought and more vulnerable than she'd imagined.

She no longer only thought of her brother's friends as just his friends, but hers, too. Maybe most important, the Lord had also given her the time and the opportunity to actually get to know Logan. Their time together had enabled her to let down her guard and have open and honest conversations with him. It had also allowed all the mishmash of feelings she'd had for him to meld into something more. Into love.

Yep, she had definitely fallen in love with Logan Clark.

Her pulse sped up slightly as she realized just how different love felt from infatuation. Whereas for most of her life she'd only thought about Logan's traits — his handsome blond hair and blue eyes, his ready smile, his gregarious nature — those things didn't have much to do with the love that had settled in her heart whenever she thought of him. Perhaps she'd fallen in love with the sum of his parts and not just his pleasing attributes.

Looking out the window again, she focused on one particularly bright star and pretended it was God gazing right down on her.

Since the time was right, she figured she might as well chat with him, even if it was from the silence of her heart.

Well, God, what am I supposed to do now? Don't get me wrong, I'm really thankful for all the gifts You've presented to me over these last few days. I know when I get back home, I'll be making some changes and handling some things differently, too.

But if there is one thing I don't think

I'm going to be able to change, it's how I feel about Logan. I love him.

She paused, staring at the star, watching it twinkle. Half hoping, she realized, that she'd suddenly hear the Lord answering her.

She didn't hear anything but Marie shifting deeper into her sleeping bag.

Because she was wide-awake now, she decided to continue. *I know in Your world, everyone is equal. You don't see differences between sinners and angels. Between people who have made a lot of mistakes, and people who have led a near-perfect life. We all matter to You. I appreciate that, too.*

She sighed. *But, um, just in case You've forgotten, a lot of people don't think Logan and I have much in common. People have concentrated on the way we dress and the differences in the way we live our lives and decided that we shouldn't plan a life together. But what if I want that after all?*

What do I do then?

Feeling kind of silly, she gazed at that star yet again, hoping against hope that He would give her a sign about what to do next.

But it was still silent.

"Hey, Trish?"

Startled, she turned. "Logan," she whispered. "I didn't hear you get up."

"I figured you didn't. You were staring pretty intently out the window," he whispered back as he knelt down onto the floor by her side. Now looking out the window, too, he frowned. "What do you see? Is something out there?"

"No. I mean, I don't think so. The wind woke me up and then I noticed the stars."

He turned his head. "So you've been staring at the stars."

"Kind of." Though she didn't think he would disapprove of her talking to the stars, she kind of liked to keep the conversation — such as it was — between herself and the Lord. "The wind blew out the storm. It's finally stopped snowing. See? The sky is clear."

He shifted so that he was sitting with his backside on the ground with his arms wrapped around his legs. She realized then that though he was wearing his wool pants, sweatshirt, and socks, he didn't have a blanket around him. "Aren't you cold?"

"Not so much." He smiled. "I'm sitting on the side of your sleeping bag. It's pretty warm right here."

"Have you been up long? I thought you were asleep."

He shrugged. "I don't know what happened. I was asleep, and then next thing I knew, I was wide awake. Just as I was going to roll over and try to go back to sleep, I noticed you sitting here." He looked at her more closely. "Are you sure you're all right?"

"Very sure. If you want to know the truth, I . . . well, I've been praying."

He tilted his head to one side. "Is that how you usually pray, staring out at the night sky?"

"No. Usually I talk out loud to the Lord, like we're having a conversation. It was kind of hard to do that here, though."

He stared at her for a long moment. "Did I interrupt you?"

Only Logan would ask such a thing! "No, I think we were finished."

"*Gut.* I would hate to think I interrupted something," he whispered.

"Would you hate it if you discovered that your conversation is waking the rest of the room up?" Harley called out.

"Oh! I'm sorry!" Mortified, Tricia covered her face with her hands.

But Logan just laughed. "Forgive us?"

"You'll be forgiven if you quiet down for a couple of hours."

"We will, but there's no need for you to embarrass Tricia like that," Logan said.

Trish groaned. Somehow, Logan had just made things worse. "Hush."

"No one wants to embarrass you, but something needed to be said," Elizabeth Ann interjected. "It's the middle of the night. Go to sleep, you two."

Reaching for her hand, Logan squeezed it. "*Gut nacht,* Tricia."

"*Gut nacht* to you, too," she said

softly. A little more loudly, she said, "Go back to sleep, Harley. I promise I'll be quiet from now on."

But she didn't hear anything as she lay back down. No doubt he was already asleep.

Taking one last look at "her" star, she smiled before closing her eyes.

Thank you, God. You've just given me everything I needed to know.

FIFTEEN

"Want to help me bring out a pitcher of lemonade?" Sarah asked me.

"Sure." I followed her into the house, blinking as my eyes tried to adjust to the dark rooms. When we got to the kitchen, Mrs. Clark and two of Sarah's younger sisters were baking cookies.

"Who are you?" Mrs. Clark asked.

"This here is Andy's sister, Tricia," Sarah said. "She's ten."

"I'm pleased to meet you, Tricia," Mrs. Clark said.

Still practically beaming from the recent win and Logan's twirl, I smiled broadly. "It's nice to meet you, too."

"Well, we made it," Logan said as Tricia was about to get in her car. "We survived the trip to the cabin in the middle of the worst snowstorm in twenty-five years."

She felt her bottom lip tremble. "We sure did. Is it weird if I admit that I'm going to miss being here?"

"*Nee.* I'm going to miss it, too.

I'm going to miss you, Tricia."

Hope surged as she stared at him, trying to memorize each feature on his face, though everything inside of her said there was no need. She'd stared at him so often over the last forty-eight hours, she knew she'd never forget every expression he'd made. "Does this mean we won't see each other for a while?"

"I don't see how we will. I mean, aren't you going back to college?"

"I'm going to finish the semester, but then I'm going to come home. I wasn't happy there. I think there are other choices for me in my future."

"Such as?"

"Such as . . . maybe us."

Just as visions of the two of them

living a long and happy future filled his head, the reality of their situation hit him square in the eye. "Tricia, you know I've been baptized, right?"

"I do. I remember the day you told me about it."

Thinking that she was still confused, Logan continued gently. "Do you know what that means, though? I've given a promise to God, my family, and myself. I'm not going to leave my faith. I'm Amish, Tricia."

"I realize that."

"Then . . ." He let his voice drift off. He didn't want to state the obvious out loud any more than he already had. Speaking about what could never be hurt too much.

"Logan, if you are going to always be Amish, I think I have some other things to study besides math, don't you?"

His mind must have been playing tricks on him, because he could have sworn she was talking about changing her life completely. "What are you saying?"

"Trish?" Elizabeth Ann yelled. "Get in that car and turn it on. We're waiting for you to follow us back."

No way was Tricia leaving right that very second. "Hold on, E. A.!"

"But the engine's running."

"I will," Tricia called out. "Please, just give me two minutes." Turning back to him, her brown eyes looked luminous. "I'm saying what you think I am, Logan. I'm willing to do whatever it takes to be with you."

"You'd consider becoming Amish?" He could hardly believe he was even asking such a thing. Could hardly believe how badly he wanted his wish to come true.

She nodded. "I know it might take years before I'm ready, but I don't mind waiting a while longer for you." She looked down at the ground before meeting his gaze again. "But the way I figure it, another year or two or three is nothing. After all, I've already been waiting for you since I was ten."

Since she was ten. An old memory suddenly surfaced. A memory of a hot and sunny summer day in his front yard. A moment when he'd given in to an impulse and twirled her in his arms and it had felt so perfect and right.

Was that what Tricia was referring to?

He opened his mouth to ask, but stopped himself just in time. It had been such a little thing. Inconsequential, really.

Standing in front of him, Tricia bit her bottom lip. "Logan, were you serious about the two of us, or did I get it all wrong?"

Even though Andy might kill him, there was no way he was going to let Tricia think their relationship was one-sided. "I was serious."

She smiled softly. "Then I'm serious about this, too."

His heart was pounding. She was staring up at him with such trust, he ached to pull her into his arms. Finally claim the lips that he'd been trying so hard not to notice for far too long.

But no matter how amazing this moment was, it wasn't the right time.

"I'm going to come by your house when your family gets back," he said. "Then we're going to talk about all of this again."

She smiled softly. "I'll be waiting for your visit."

Suddenly, he didn't care whether it was the right time or not. He needed to hold her. To touch her. To do something to seal the promises that they'd just made. Unclenching one of his hands, he reached out and brushed her hair away from her face.

"Tricia Warner, you get in your car now or I'm calling your brother!"

Eyes wide, Tricia stepped away. "I've got to go. Marie isn't kidding." Looking sheepish, she reached out and clasped his hand. "Thank you again for coming to save me."

He wrapped his hand around hers and squeezed it. "I'd do it again in a heartbeat. Always." Looking beyond her, he sighed. "Come on. Marie's right. It is time to go." Especially since it looked as if they had a lot more ahead of the two of them in the future.

Sixteen

After handing me four mason jars, Sarah picked up the lemonade pitcher and headed out.

Feeling awkward again, I followed.

Then, just before we went outside again, she turned to me. "You know you're *Englisch* and Logan's Amish, right?"

"Of course."

"Then you ought to remember that we can all be friends but never anything more."

Everything she said made sense, but I didn't believe it. Even back then I'd known that what actually mattered was how people acted, not who they were.

All that is why I lifted my chin, looked Sarah Clark right in the eye, and said, "I don't know about that. I mean, never is a really long time."

"You need to stop worrying, Andy," Tricia said for at least the third or fourth time. "I'm home, the cabin is locked tight, Logan and his horses are back at his place, and the rest of your friends are home safe now, too. It's over."

Andy gripped his cell phone tighter as he tried his best to not say something he would later regret. But it was hard. Only his sister would act like he was overreacting about the fact that four of his friends had to move heaven and earth in order to make sure she was home safe.

When Andy finally felt like he could talk without yelling, he said, "It's not as simple as that, Trish. Just because you're home safe, it doesn't mean that this whole episode has been forgotten."

"What do you want me to say? Thank you? I've told you and Logan and Marie and Harley and Elizabeth thank you multiple times."

"I know you're grateful."

"But?"

"But you don't want me to finish my thought."

"No, I do," she countered, impatience lifting her voice. "Tell me what you're really thinking."

"I'm thinking that it's unfair of you to think that we're all supposed to keep your secret," he replied. "To assume that Logan Clark didn't miss multiple days of work. That Marie and the rest of them didn't rearrange their whole schedules to save your rear end."

"I never said that I thought they did. And I'm not asking you to keep the secret."

"So you are fine with me telling Mom and Dad?"

"If it means that you are going to stop making me feel guilty, I am very fine with that."

"I might just tell them everything," he warned. He knew he was acting like a jerk, but honestly, his little sister had to start making better choices. What if he hadn't been able to take her phone call when she'd first called? Something really bad could have happened to her.

"If you do, I hope it feels great and freeing. Do whatever you need to do. In fact, Logan said that . . . never mind."

There was something different in her voice. Concerned, Andy tried to place it. What was it? A new warmth? "What did Logan say?"

"Nothing that you need to know. It's between him and me."

Him and her? "Wait a minute. Logan and I are best friends."

"I know that, but maybe he and I are close now, too."

There was something new in his little sister's voice. Something he didn't quite understand but that was starting to worry him. "What is that supposed to mean?"

"It means that I think it's time I got off the phone."

He wanted to argue with her, attempt to explain again how he was feeling, but he knew he wasn't going to win that battle. "Fine."

"I'll call again soon, Andy."

"Wait!"

"What?"

"I love you, Tricia. I'm glad you're home safe."

When she spoke again, her voice was rough sounding. "I love you back, brother. Thank you for helping me so much. I would be lost without you."

"Luckily you won't ever have to worry about that," he said, finally able to smile.

"Bye again," she said around a chuckle before disconnecting.

After pressing End as well, Andy sat down on one of the lounge chairs and finally allowed his body to relax. Tricia wasn't in danger. She was fine. And though she had needed a little bit of help, she'd taken care of everything without him.

Maybe if one day he wasn't there for her, she would be just fine on her own.

"Andy?"

"Yes?" He turned to see his mother approach.

"What's been going on with you?" she asked as she sat down on the chair next to him, her navy jersey dress flowing around her knees.

For a second, he took the time to realize that his mother was still very pretty. When he was little, he'd never thought about her looks. When he'd gotten to high school, her youthful looks kind of embarrassed him. More than one guy had teased him about having a hot mom. But now he realized that her looks were simply a part of her, just as his father's studious nature was a part of him.

"What do you mean?"

She glared at him. "Oh, please. Tricia might get away with playing dumb from time to time, but you've never been good at it. I'm talking about all the intense phone conversations you've been having. Practically every day I've seen you on the phone, your expression so intent, like there was something really bothering you. What's been wrong?" She held up a hand. "And don't tell me it's work. No one looks that concerned about work unless he or she is worried about getting fired." Her eyes widened.

"Oh, no. Is that it?"

"No. My job is just fine."

"Is it Kalie?"

"No."

"Then what is it?"

"The truth is, I've been talking to Tricia." Even though he didn't feel good about betraying her, he liked keeping these secrets even less. If he didn't share what had happened, chances were pretty good that they were all going to come back to bite him. He hated lies and he could never remember them, either.

"Tricia?" Looking both aggravated and pained, she exhaled. "You've been talking to her that much? Oh my word. What has she done now?"

And just like that, he changed his

mind.

Tricia had been right. She'd done so many goofy things over the years, their parents were kind of over giving her the benefit of the doubt. Now they automatically assumed the worst.

If their parents got wind of this latest mess, they'd freak out. She'd made a pretty bad decision and she could've gotten hurt or in a car accident. But instead of sympathizing with her, they'd most likely chalk it up to another silly episode. Say it was another example of how she really wasn't capable of doing much on her own. Next thing Trish knew, she'd be leaving Bowling Green early and moving back home into her old bedroom.

Besides, he'd promised her he'd keep her secret. Maybe that counted for more than even the consequences.

"Trish hasn't done anything, Mom," he said, hoping that he sounded kind of put out. "I mean, not besides feeling disappointed that she didn't come on vacation with us. I've been talking to her so much because she's been kind of lonely."

"That's it?"

He did his best to look affronted. "What? Isn't that enough? You know how empty the house can get. I'm sure she's regretting her choice and wishing she could have just driven down here."

"Thank goodness she didn't. She

could've gotten stuck in some of that nasty weather. Then what would she have done?"

Feeling like the lies and half-truths were coming far too easily now, he shrugged. "I don't know. Though I do know that you won't have to wonder. She's fine."

"Yes, of course." Crossing her legs, she leaned back in her chair. "I'm sorry. I sounded pretty harsh, didn't I? I don't know why I always assume the worst about that girl. She does so much right. I need to focus on that more." She shook her head. "No, I need to tell her that more often."

"She knows you love her, Mom."

"I hope so."

"She does. I know she does."

Thinking of all the escapades Tricia had been involved in over the years, he added, "Mom, I don't think you should be too hard on yourself. I mean, Tricia really has given you reason to think the worst is coming a time or two."

"I guess that's true." She pressed her lips together. "I hate the thought of her being home alone and sad. I wonder why she never called Dad or me? I would've been happy to chat with her."

Fervently wishing he weren't in the middle of this convoluted conversation, Andy paused. He needed to attempt to navigate it without going behind Tricia's back or making his mother feel worse than she already did.

He settled for the truth. "Mom, if she'd called you and told you she was bored and lonely, what would you have said?"

Looking sheepish, she said, "I would like to say I would have been understanding and sympathetic, but I have a feeling we both know better. Knowing me, I would have gotten on her case about staying home." Drumming her fingers on her thigh, she sighed. "Which would, of course, have made Trish feel even worse."

"I'm glad she called me."

"I feel bad, though. You've been putting in so much overtime at work. Dad and I wanted you to enjoy yourself, not worry about your sister the whole time."

"I have enjoyed myself." But as far as worrying about Trish? Well, they didn't even know the half of it! "I'm glad she called me. It's good to feel needed."

"She's always needed you, Andy. Just like you've always looked out for her, just like you've always looked out for everyone."

"Come on, Mom. You know that's not true."

"I think it is. I think that maybe you also aren't thinking of yourself the way others see you." Shifting again, she kicked her legs out in front of her, crossing her ankles. "Why, I remember when you were just six or seven. Remember when you first went over to Mrs. Kurt's house and made friends with all the kids there?"

"I do. I went from being upset that you were sending me to a babysitter to never wanting the weekend to come."

"I heard from the other parents that the rest of those kids felt the same way. What you built with them, with the Eight, was special. Tricia never did feel as close to the rest of them."

"She liked being near you and at the office day care. I would've hated every minute."

"I knew that," she said softly. "What I'm trying to say is that I'm not surprised that you took Tricia's burdens on as your own. You've done that for your friends from time to time."

"That was different. God intended for them to be my best friends." He believed it, too. On paper, it didn't make sense that so many kids from such varied backgrounds would ever forge such a bond.

"If God intended that, then he also intended for you to be the boy to pull everyone together and make a cohesive group."

He didn't like how she was making it seem as if there wouldn't be the Eight without him. "I don't know about that."

"I do. Each member of your group is unique and special. I firmly believe that. But not each member was meant to be the leader. That was you." She smiled

softly. "And here you are now, helping Tricia get through a difficult
time. I guess you've become her
leader, too."

"I don't think that's true, but
thanks."

"Does she need anything before
we get back in two days?"

"No, she's fine." Thanks to Logan, Marie, Harley, and E. A.

She got up. "All right, then, I'll
try not to worry. Oh! I actually
came out here for a reason, and
that's to tell you to get ready to go
to dinner. Your dad wants to leave
in fifteen minutes."

"I'll be ready."

She smiled at him, delighted, then
turned to walk back into the condo,
running her hand across the top of

his head as she did.

When he was alone again, he got to his feet and walked over to the balcony and rested his elbows on it. Right below was the condo association's pool. Four or five people were lying in lounge chairs below him.

Lifting his chin, he scanned the parking lot just beyond the pool area. Then the grassy slope, along with the gap through the fancy landscaping to where a series of steps was cut into the slope, zigzagging through the space and eventually popping out the other side. On the beach.

The wide expanse, stretching for miles in either direction, sloping toward the banks and the surf.

Eventually disappearing into the murky blue waters. And beyond.

He loved standing in this spot, gazing into the distance, letting his mind drift, reminding himself that he was just one person in a very big world.

Really, when it came down to it, he hardly mattered at all. Until he thought of his sister and his friends. Of the Eight.

A sense of peace surrounded him, and the headache that seemed to be his constant companion of late finally lessened. Easing the depression that had seemed to take hold of him more often than not these days.

He shook it off.

No, right now, at this minute,

everything was right in his world. His sister was safe and happy. His friends were, too. He was standing in the sun, and its heat was warming his skin. He relaxed, allowed his eyes to unfocus. Allowed the rest of his senses to acknowledge everything. The sights. The smells. The warmth.

The way he was free of pain.

It was almost as if God Himself was reaching out and soothing him, reminding Andy that He was there, that he had never been alone, just like Andy had tried so hard to always be there for Tricia. Just like the Lord had always been there for Tricia, too; she had just never realized it.

This feeling of well-being that had

settled over him, combined with the warmth of the sun and his hope for the future, raised his spirits. He was good.

Right now? He didn't need another thing.

"Andy? You ready?"

He turned. Saw his parents through the screen of the sliding door. Waiting for him.

"Yeah. I'm ready, Dad," he replied. For the first time in a long while, he felt ready for anything the future had to offer. He held on to that feeling and held on tight.

ACKNOWLEDGMENTS

Dear Reader,

I hope you enjoyed *Friends to the End.* Like Tricia in this novella, I've been experiencing a few growing pains myself! I was thrilled to be given this opportunity to begin a new series with a new publisher. It's not often that a writer gets to make a leap like that, and I'm very grateful for the support that my editor, Marla Daniels, and the whole team at Gallery and Simon & Schuster have already given me.

I've been playing with the idea of setting a series in Walnut Creek for some time. Walnut Creek, in the heart of Holmes County, Ohio, is very familiar to me, and setting a series of novels there feels like coming home.

While I had the first three chapters of *The Patient One* written for some time, I always felt that something was missing! I have Marla to thank for the addition of this novella. Her guidance helped give Andy Warner a voice. I hope as you continue the series that you will also be glad to have gotten to know Andy.

No letter of acknowledgment would be complete without thanking you, my readers. It's because of y'all that I was able to begin my tenth Amish series. Thank you for putting your trust in me.

If you get a chance, let me know what you think! I love to hear from y'all.

With my blessings and my thanks,
Shelley

ABOUT THE AUTHOR

Shelley Shepard Gray is the *New York Times* and *USA TODAY* best-selling author of more than sixty novels, translated into multiple languages. She lives in southern Ohio with her family and writes full time.

The employees of Thorndike Press hope you have enjoyed this Large Print book. All our Thorndike, Wheeler, and Kennebec Large Print titles are designed for easy reading, and all our books are made to last. Other Thorndike Press Large Print books are available at your library, through selected bookstores, or directly from us.

For information about titles, please call:
    (800) 223-1244

or visit our website at:
    gale.com/thorndike

To share your comments, please write:
    Publisher
    Thorndike Press
    10 Water St., Suite 310
    Waterville, ME 04901